Hill Street Clues

A Josephine Stuart Mystery

by

Joyce Oroz

For information, email **Cozy Cat Press**, cozycatpress@aol.com or visit our website at: www.cozycatpress.com

ISBN: 978-1-946063-60-1

Printed in the United States of America

1 2 3 4 5 6 7 8 9 10

I want to thank my friends and family for supporting my writing habit.
Without them, it would truly be a lonely sport.

I happen to have the most wonderful editor, Tomiko Edmiston,
helping me to bring another book to its finish.
Thank you so much, dear friend.

And warm thank you's to my wonderful husband
for his input and patience.

And many thanks to Patricia Rockwell at Cozy Cat Press
for publishing my newest mystery.

I love being in the "Cozy Cat" family.

Books in the Josephine Stuart Mystery Series

Secure the Ranch
Read My Lipstick
Shaking In Her Flip Flops
Beetles In the Boxcar
Cuckoo Clock Caper
Roller Rubout
Scent of a $windle
Who Murdered Mary Christmas
Pushing up Daisy
Hill Street Clues

Other Books by Joyce Oroz

Annie Gets Her Bounce
Muraling For Fun And Profit

.

Chapter 1

There were times when I couldn't wait to tell my best friend Alicia Quintana and my fiancé David Galaz, what was on my mind. But some things needed to be kept secret. Things I don't even want to think about, like the particulars surrounding the death of my neighbor Mrs. Oeblick.

Friday night I agreed to help Alicia paint a sign for her son's soccer league. Saturday morning, as we painted over capital letters carved in relief across a six-foot slab of pure redwood securely mounted on two iron legs at the entrance to Lakeview Park, we talked about day-to-day trivia until the subject of my neighbor came up.

"Jo, did you know Mrs. Oeblick?" Alicia gave me a sideways glance.

"I ran into her a few times over the last ten years. She was quiet, maybe because her English wasn't very good. Definitely an 'old-country' lady wearing a knitted shawl and a big accent. Mostly I remember her long crooked nose and little white whiskers on her chin."

Mrs. Oeblick lived with her sixty-year-old son, Jason Oeblick, in a two-story house at the end of Otis Road, just seven houses and thirty-five acres past my little adobe home planted on five acres of grass, oak trees, wild lilac and hungry gophers.

"Jo, you missed a spot." Alicia pointed to the *E* at the end of Watsonville.

"Thanks, Allie. Ever since I turned fifty, I can't concentrate like I used to. Sign painting isn't so bad, but

I'd rather be painting murals. I can't wait to start our new project." Thanks to an anonymous donation attached to a mural request, the city of Gilroy was able to secure a contract with my mural company, Wildbrush Murals.

"Have you seen the library yet?" I asked.

"No, I hardly ever go to Gilroy," Alicia said. "Just a visit to the Outlets once a year to buy school clothes for Trigger."

Alicia's ten-year-old son, Trigger, would go far in life with his good looks, sharp mind and natural sense of humor. He loved soccer and baseball, which was the perfect excuse for his father, UC Santa Cruz Professor Ernie Quintana, to volunteer his time coaching.

A chilly November breeze ruffled my shoulder-length auburn hair, as yellow and amber leaves fluttered to the ground.

Alicia pushed a clump of silky black hair away from her beautiful light brown Latin face, while painting a perfect letter *O*.

"Did I tell you how much Trigger likes fifth grade? Actually, he's in love with his teacher, Ms. Tilly," she giggled, as she reloaded her brush with inky black paint.

"That's an interesting name."

"It's short for Mrs. Tillsdale," Alicia said, as she expertly brushed on the last three letters of "League." She dropped her brush into a plastic cup of water, tipped her head to one side and squinted at the overall signage.

"So, are we finished?" I asked, gazing far beyond the park lawn, across the valley floor at an unsettled sky and a bank of black clouds on the horizon.

Alicia nodded. "The sign looks good—thanks for the help. Jo, you didn't tell me what happened to Mrs. Oeblick."

"Let's just say it wasn't a natural death, with a big knot on the top of her head and a broken neck. In the newspaper it said Jason found her lying on a concrete walkway under her bedroom balcony."

"Didn't you tell me they had horses?"

"Yeah, but I haven't seen any sign of horses recently."

"Do you think Jason did it?" Alicia said, as she loaded the paint box into my trusty red Mazda pickup. I hoisted a canvas bag full of empty paint containers, a satchel of brushes and a folded tarp into the truck bed and pulled the metal top down snug.

"No. I only met him once, but I don't think Jason is the type who'd kill his mother. Besides, he has an alibi, and everyone tells me he's a nice guy. I didn't even know the Oeblicks had horses until about a year ago when I happened to see Jason driving down Otis in a green WildWest Nursery pickup truck pulling a horse trailer. As you know, I don't have a view of Otis from my house; I just happened to be at the end of the driveway getting the mail when he drove by. I remember he wore a cowboy hat and a big droopy white mustache, looking like a character from an old western movie."

"Is Jason's dad still alive?" Alicia asked as she climbed into the passenger seat.

"He's alive all right. David told me that Mr. Oeblick is living in Gilroy with his sixty-year-old hanky-panky ex-daughter-in-law who—get this—used to be his son Jason's wife." I snorted and rolled my eyes. "Rumor has it that Mr. Oeblick is quite the lady's man."

Alicia tilted her head and squinted at me. "Is that the truth or just a rumor?"

"I'm sure Jason wishes it was just a rumor." I fired up the engine and we headed for Alicia's house at the edge of Drew Lake on the eastside of Watsonville, a town known as "the salad bowl of the world." People always said, "If it won't grow in Watsonville, it won't grow." I always said, "Plant it at my house and for sure it won't grow." The only time the struggling marigolds in my window box had water was when it rained. Lucky for them, it was already November. They wouldn't have to wait long for life-sustaining rain water. Or, if I remembered, I could drench them with the hose.

After dropping Alicia at her house, I decided to stop at my favorite grocery store. It was four o'clock in the afternoon and ominously dark clouds had already gobbled up the last bit of blue sky. I parked the truck, rolled a cart into the store and pushed it up and down the aisles gathering dog treats for Solow and basic food for me. My basket was half full when I walked up to Robert, my young freckled friend who was stocking the dairy case, his big blue apron too long and narrow for his body type.

"Hey, Josephine, nice colorful outfit! His blue eyes twinkled. "Some of those paint clothes you wear are real trend-setters."

"At least I don't have to wear a big blue apron to work," I grinned.

Robert, always wise for his age and well-read, looked over his shoulder at me and asked if I had known Mrs. Oeblick.

"Barely; just ran into her a couple times over the years."

Robert straightened a row of cottage cheese containers with a practiced push of his hand. "Do you think her son did it?"

"I haven't looked into it…much."

"Right! Josephine, you don't fool me. You're already trying to figure out who murdered Mrs. Oeblick."

"I think it would be easy to blame Jason. In fact, I believe someone wanted him to be blamed. I drove up to their house a couple days after the murder just to look at the horses…you know, to see if they were being fed. But the horses were gone. Jason seemed like a nice guy."

"My friend the snoop," Robert laughed.

"Okay, I admit I'm curious. How are the strawberries today?"

"Small, but the blueberries are fabulous and so are the red grapes."

"Thanks, Robert," I said over my shoulder, as I left the dairy aisle and pushed my cart toward a bevy of freshly picked berries and grapes. My young friend was an expert on many subjects and knew produce like the back of his chubby little hands. However, I didn't tell Robert everything I knew about the Oeblicks, like the personal information I had gleaned from my impromptu visit with Jason. Like the fact that Mrs. Oeblick had been suffering with cancer and was given four months to live, and the fact that she sold the house out from under her own son. Jason had told me he didn't know what she was up to until the sale was already in escrow. It didn't seem right to discuss these sad family matters with Robert.

Driving home with three bags of groceries in the truck bed, I wondered if I should stop by the Oeblick place and see if Jason needed anything. I figured the frozen foods would keep everything else cold. So instead of turning up my driveway, I kept going to the end of the road plus a hundred-foot stretch of concrete driveway that ended in a circle.

I parked the truck opposite the front door entrance. If Jason was home, his black pickup truck must be in the garage. There was only one way to find out.

A little white dog with perky ears and a limp ran up to my truck, barking.

I climbed down from my seat and slammed the door. Between the barking dog and the door slamming, Jason must have known I was there. Up three wide steps to the front door, I rang the bell, worked the brass knocker and finally peeked through the window.

"Oops!" I was face to face with Jason on the other side of the glass.

A moment later, the front door opened.

"Quiet, Charlie," Jason said.

The little white dog quietly circled my legs and shot through the door, disappearing into the front room.

"Hello, Jasmin," Jason said, sucking blood from a bleeding thumb.

"Josephine," I said, shuddering as a cool breeze wafted across the back of my neck.

"Chilly today," he said, looking past me at the darkening sky. "Would you like to come in?"

"Ah, sure. Did you know there's blood on your shirt?" I said, stepping into a tile entry with barn wood paneling to my right and left.

Jason ran fingers through his short grey hair and straightened a Garth Brooks tee shirt, bloodstain and all, over his middle-aged mid-section. For a sixty-year-old, he looked pretty fit. He led me into the living room and motioned for me to sit down on one of the two big brown leather couches.

"Jason, I just wanted you to know that the whole neighborhood sends its regrets." Actually, David had expressed concern for Jason, and I sort of threw the rest of our neighbors into the mix hoping to ease the pain I saw in Jason's dark eyes.

"Thank you, Jasmin...."

"It's Josephine. By the way, I have three bags of groceries outside in my truck. Is there anything you need? Eggs, coffee, dog food...?"

"No, but thanks for asking. The only thing I need is help with the nursery," Jason said under his breath, stroking his silky white mustache thoughtfully. "Know anyone who wants a job? Two of my employees walked off the job when they read the newspaper account of my mother's murder. I guess they didn't believe in me." His eyes went from sad to mad for a split second.

"I don't know anyone looking for a job, and I'm afraid my mural work doesn't qualify me for working in a nursery." My eyes wandered around the room to at least a dozen framed twelve by sixteen-inch bucking bronco cowboy photographs. Every picture featured a man with a mustache, Jason in his prime.

Jason chuckled. "All you would be doing is ringing up the sales—no big deal, and I'll pay top dollar. To tell you the truth, I'm exhausted. I'm running the business short-handed and trying to get this house packed up."

"That's right; you told me she sold the house," I said, feeling sad about his situation. I noticed a dozen or more stacked boxes lined up against the far wall.

"Yeah, Mom was pretty old and forgetful. My sister offered to buy the house." Jason's jaw tightened. "Fern offered what Mom thought was a lot of money— but it wasn't even close to prices these days."

"You're really in a spot."

"Yeah, having the police breathing down my neck isn't helping either."

"I'd love to help out, but...."

"Well, neighbor, don't worry your pretty head. I'll find someone." Jason looked at the floor.

"Any idea who killed your mom?" I asked, as an idea crossed my mind—a way to get information on the crime, and possibly figure out who perpetrated it.

"Nope." His eyes welled up. He looked away.

"I have a mural job at the end of this month," I said, thinking out loud. "But maybe I could help you out until you find a permanent employee." I watched as Jason's worry lines dissolved and his eyes focused on me. His warm smile could have melted masonry.

"Do you know my fiancé, David Galaz? He lives in the ranch-style house next to my adobe."

"Yeah, I met him once—nice guy."

Jason's brave smile held. He didn't appear to be a lecher or an ax murderer, so I asked when my first day at the nursery would be. He said he had help for Sunday, but Monday I was urgently needed at eight a.m. He said he had to deliver trees to San Carlos that morning plus lantana and half a dozen olive trees to Fresno in the afternoon.

No wonder he had dark circles under is eyes.

"Do you need help bandaging that thumb?" I asked.

"Nah, I can take care of it. I've broken almost every bone in my body ridin' broncos. Guess I can deal with a paper cut." He walked me to the door.

"Do you still have horses on the property?"

"Nope, my rodeo days are over."

"Did you know that your little dog is limping?"

"Yeah, someone kicked him. See you Monday, Jasmin...I mean Josephine."

"You can call me Jo." I climbed into my truck, followed the circle and rolled past thirteen neighboring properties. Turning up my gravel driveway, I pulled to a stop next to David's car. I smiled to myself when I saw the porch light on and smelled wood smoke coming from the chimney. David always did the nicest things. The front door opened and my favorite guys came out to greet me. I climbed out of my seat, hugged David and patted Solow's long basset physique.

"Josie, I just got a call from a buddy of mine. He's coming over to pick up some dried apricots. See ya tomorrow." He gave me a peck on my cheek and drove away in his late model red Miata. No invitation to go next door and meet his buddy. Just a peck and goodbye, leaving me to bring in the groceries, make dinner and watch a movie all alone. But before the movie started, I called Alicia.

"Jo, what's going on?"

"I still can't believe David went home and left me alone on a Saturday night."

"You're crying to the choir, my friend; Ernie's at a meeting at the college tonight. Something about students burning books because they don't feel safe? I don't get it, but the teachers are all in a huff, looking for a way to mollify those crazy kids."

"Allie, you'll never guess what I'm doing for the next couple weeks."

"I give up. What are you doing?"

"I'm going to work at a nursery...."

"Jo, it better be nursery school because everyone on the planet knows more about plants than you."

"It's the WildWest Nursery in Gilroy, and I know about marigolds and...."

"Your marigolds are half dead from lack of food and water."

"Another good reason to work there. I'll be learning how to take care of all kinds of plants."

Alicia snorted. "You don't fool me, Jo, The nursery happens to be the Oeblick family business. You're going to work there so you can find out who killed Mrs. Oeblick."

"And that would be one more reason to go to work at the nursery," I joyfully said to my dear smart aleck friend.

"What if Jason murdered his mother? Are you taking your pepper spray with you?" she asked, her voice showing actual concern.

I thought about Jason for a moment. He was easy on the eyes, in fairly good condition for his age, sounded sincere and looked like he could use some help. On top of that, he had a perfect alibi for the day his mother was killed. He said he had been delivering plants to a ranch in Santa Barbara that day.

Chapter 2

California typically receives its first seasonal rain in November. Sure enough, it was the second Monday in November when the first storm muddied the earth and ruined my plans for a pleasant day helping out at the WildWest Nursery. Because Sunday had been a perfectly sunny day, Monday was an unpleasant surprise. I had imagined myself ringing up purchases, chatting with customers and tidying up the gift shop. I didn't imagine digging a trench to keep water from washing away the east end of the nursery's gravel parking lot, and I never imagined how cold a three-sided gift shop could get. And I never ever imagined a woman employee like Bea.

"What's the matta, missy, never worked outdoors before?" Bea said, blowing smoke out her puggish nostrils.

I had asked Beatrice, Jason's number one and only employee, questions and seldom received satisfactory answers. Her dinged up off-white compact car, parked in front of a long white stucco wall, had a bumper full of colorful peeling sarcastic stickers.

Beatrice liked to sit in the gift shop drinking coffee and smoking extra long cigarettes under the "No Smoking" sign tacked to the yellowed plaster wall. She managed to stay clear of the cash register positioned directly under one of three small leaks in the roof.

Bea finally dowsed her cigarette butt in one of the pots I had set out to catch the leaks. The middle-aged woman wore denim overalls over a bulky grey sweater.

I would have gladly traded my favorite tennis shoes for her big yellow rubber boots. My jeans were already soaked and the watermark was quickly moving north toward my knees. My lightweight shirt and jacket were useless in the windy wetness of WildWest Nursery.

Finally, at ten o'clock our first customer arrived.

I walked up to her and asked if she needed help.

"Do you have any more yellow pansies? I underestimated. It seems I need one more," the well-dressed middle-aged woman said. She collapsed her umbrella and hooked it over one arm.

I looked at Bea who was checking her phone. Again.

"Okay," I smiled. "Let's see what we have. We'll just walk to the place where you found your first batch of pansies, and when you see a pansy, just let me know." We headed outside, she with an umbrella, me with dripping wet hair. I followed her along the muddy path until she pointed to a wheelbarrow displaying several dozen little potted monkey-faced plants. The woman pointed to the yellow ones. I picked one up and handed it to her. She inspected it closely as if she were looking for flaws in a four-carat diamond. Finally, she said she'd take it.

I rang up the $2.99 purchase and she drove away.

"Bea, what do we do now?"

"Just a minute, I need a smoke break."

And I needed a break from her smoke, so I checked out the connecting restroom and storeroom. The former was mighty small, and the latter had a large footprint. The over-sized tin shed was as big as a barn and held everything from ladders to trimmers to mowers to sacks of fertilizer to shovels, hoes and rakes. I had just begun organizing the cutters and trimmers when I heard tires on gravel. As I entered the gift shop, I noticed that Bea's large lazy presence was missing.

A gentleman wearing a full-length raincoat wandered among the potted something-or-others. He saw me coming and explained that he needed two Monterey pine trees in the ten-gallon size.

Imagining a Christmas tree in a ten-gallon container, I was just about to ask a really stupid question when the man walked up to a very long row of potted trees. The pots and trees ranged in size. He picked out two long-needled pines and pointed to the one I was to carry. Not only was it muddy, it was heavy. I groaned.

"Oh, sorry, I thought you worked here," he said.

"I do. Don't worry; I got it," I said, as I hoisted the heavy pot into my arms and slopped through the cold puddles, unable to see where I was going because my face was immersed in tree branches. A pine needle went up my nose causing me to shake my head, which caused my feet to slip out from under me. By the time I pulled the tree and myself to a standing position, the customer was approaching the parking lot fifty feet ahead.

We leaned the trees against a bench near the gift shop. I bent down to examine one of them for a price.

"The price is right here on the pot," the man said, pointing to a white sticker with black print.

"Thanks."

Glad to be back under a roof, never mind that it leaked, I rang up the trees and watched the man insert his credit card. Finally, I made a sixty-dollar sale. Things were looking up.

The phone rang.

Bea arrived in time to answer it, "WildWest Nursery, how can I help ya?" She rolled her eyes and grinned. "No problem, I'll have um there in an hour."

She hung up and looked at me. "One of our regulars needs sixteen five-gallon oaks right away. Just stick 'um in the back of the truck and drive um to 545 Hanover Street in Milpitas. I'll ring um up while you load."

"Okay, five oaks in sixteen-gallon...."

"No, ya got it wrong," Bea crabbed. "Sixteen trees in five-gallon pots. You're gonna have to pay attention, girl." She pointed to the east side of the nursery where I'd just come from.

Rows and rows of baby and half-grown trees stood at attention, rainwater glittering on their happy little leaves. The puddles didn't matter anymore, since my shoes and jeans were already soaked. I trudged down the rows of trees, reading labels and hoping to come upon some oak trees.

"Jo? Lookin' for something?" Jason said, looking nice and dry under his beige cowboy hat.

"I need five...I mean sixteen oaks in five gallon buckets."

"Right there!" Jason pointed to two long rows of baby oak trees, the first in line just a couple feet from where I stood. "You need to go back to the parking lot and get one of those big flat-bed carts to put the trees on, and then run 'em over to that delivery van by the gift shop. I'd help you, but I just got back from San Carlos. Now I have to load up some olive trees and get on the road to Fresno. I'll be using the big delivery truck. Need any help with the GPS?"

"Oh, that, sure...here's the address."

He looked at my note. "No worries; we do a lot of business with these people," he said. "I'll fix it for you before I go."

I tried not to show my feelings of trepidation when it came to driving unfamiliar vehicles in rainstorms, in unfamiliar towns like Milpitas. I was a painter, an artist—not a truck driver.

"Josephine, I can hear your teeth chattering. Why don't you grab a company jacket? Bea will show you where they are."

We trudged back to the carts stationed outside the gift shop. Jason picked one out for me while I asked Bea for a jacket. No wonder his other employees walked off the job, having to deal with Bea's attitude. I was sorely tempted to do the same. But a promise was a promise, so I snuggled into the big green jacket with the company yellow logo on the back.

It took all my strength to pull the flat-bed cart east along the now familiar muddy path, heft eight baby oaks onto the cart, haul them fifty yards, drop them off next to the van and then do it all again with eight more trees.

Ducking into the gift shop, I asked Bea for keys to the van because I was leaving for Milpitas just as soon as we got the trees loaded.

"We?" Bea laughed. "I have back trouble. Better hurry, the landscaper needs those trees by two and it's already one-thirty." With that warning out of the way, she sat back and lit a cigarette.

Even on a sunny day with high speed and low traffic, I knew that Milpitas was a good forty minutes northeast of Gilroy. I loaded the van as fast as I could, slid into the front seat, studied the basic dashboard and decided I'd probably be able to drive the vehicle. The radio was tuned to country music and the rain had let up, both good signs.

Charging north on Highway 101, I sang along with Justin and Dustin and Brad and Billy. The heater warmed my feet but periodically I had to wipe condensation off the windshield with a cotton glove I found in the glove box. Amazing. So that's why it's called a glove box.

"Turn right at the next exit," a loud female voice startled me out of my daydream about a recent visit with David.

I waited for more instructions. She didn't let me down.

Since I eventually made it to my destination with no mistakes, I decided there might be a future for GPS. I also knew that my friends had been using it for years—actually, I was the only dinosaur around.

"Oh my gosh," I said to myself as a long driveway bordered with palm trees looped and ended in front of a two-story mansion surrounded on three sides by fenced pastures and grazing horses. But most surprising was the big green delivery truck from WildWest Nursery already parked there by the house. I rolled down my window.

"Hey, Jo, you made decent time," Jason smiled.

"I thought you said you were going to Fresno...."

"I was. Got an emergency call from this location. One of their palm trees has an infection and they're worried that the whole batch might be sick. I'll go to Fresno tomorrow."

"It wasn't a bad drive up here after the rain quit," I said, climbing out of my seat and waiting for instructions. I heard voices and looked toward the back of the van. Two men were already unloading the trees. The rear doors slammed, and Jason told me to head back to Gilroy. Wow, just like that. No offer of hot tea or a restroom break.

I was within ten miles of the nursery when I noticed a flashing red light on the dashboard. According to the gauge, the gas tank was beyond empty. I took the third Morgan Hill exit and two blocks later, the motor sputtered and quit. I turned right and the van slowly rolled into a gas station. It stopped only five feet from the closest pump, but the hose wouldn't stretch that far no matter how hard I pulled.

I walked into the "jiffy-food" market, stopped at the register and received a blank stare from the man behind the counter, also the only person in the building.

"Sorry, ma'am, I can't leave my register."

"Yeah, don't leave those crowds of people," I growled to myself.

Stepping outside, I must have looked like I was in terrible trouble, because four teenage boys left their SUV featuring a ski rack full of snowboards, and asked if I needed help. My mouth dropped open and before I could say, "Yes," they were lined up across the back of the van waiting for me to put it in neutral and release the handbrake.

As the nursery van rolled into position at the first gas pump, I braked and climbed out of my seat.

"Hey, guys, thank you!" I shouted as they headed back to their vehicle.

One of the boys lagged behind. "We wa...want to thank you...."

"What? Thank me?" I said.

"Yeh, we be..be..belong to the Bo..Boys Club in Gilroy. You always give time and mo..money." He blushed. "Me..me..means a lot to us."

The "father figure" driving the SUV waited for the last boy to climb in, and took off for snow country. Two other SUV's packed with boys in the back seats and adults in the front, followed close behind. I smiled at the thought of so much fun and adventure ahead of them.

Sticking my credit card in the designated slot, I tried to decide how much gas I would put in my employer's van. As the gas wooshed into the tank, I stared across the street at nothing, thinking about the boy's sweet thank you. "Oops!" I groaned, as the hose handle jerked and clicked, halting the flow of gasoline. I had planned to put ten dollars worth in the tank in case Jason didn't pay me back. I hadn't planned to pump fifty-five dollars worth. Oh well, what was done was done.

By the time I arrived at WildWest Nursery, my feet were dry and I was hungry as a bear fresh out of hibernation. But the real bear was Bea, crabbing about a customer scraping their car against the cart I'd left in the parking lot.

"Bea, are you sure the customer wasn't texting on her phone when she hit the cart?"

She took a drag on her cigarette. "How do I know? I was here, where I'm supposed to be," she snapped, "while you and Jason were gallivanting all over the place."

"Okay, next time you deliver the plants while I stay here." I went to the warehouse and organized the shovels, rakes and hoes. Hearing the crunch of gravel outside, I entered the gift shop and watched Bea order her lunch from a taco vending truck in the parking lot.

"Thanks for letting me know, Ms. Bea," I said to myself as my tummy growled. A young man took my order and minutes later handed me a steaming hot tamale with rice and beans, all nestled in a small cardboard container.

A compact car pulled to a stop next to the taco truck. An elderly woman locked her car and followed me into the gift shop. She asked a million questions about succulents, types of soil, and pot sizes while Bea ate her lunch and mine sat by the register going cold. If only I could have thought about her questions clearly, without the distraction of tamale aroma and hunger pains.

"Thank you, dear, for trying to answer my questions. I think I'll just go with my instincts and buy two dozen of these cute little succulents and two dozen of those darling orange pots. You see, I'm having the family over for Thanksgiving dinner in a few weeks. I want everyone to go home with a sweet little treasure."

"That's very thoughtful of you," I said, putting the plants into their pots and the pots into cardboard flats. She paid for them out of a sock full of cash. I made three trips carrying one flat at a time to the trunk of her car.

"Thank you, dear," she said. "I always bring my business here because you people do such good work in the community." She backed up, cranked the wheel and barely missed hitting a cart on her way to the road.

I pushed the cart closer to the gift shop, entered the three-sided building and ate my cold tamale. When I finished, Bea looked at my empty plate. "If you need a microwave, it's in the warehouse."

"Yeah, maybe next time. How long have you worked here...?"

"Off and on for two years. Jason's my brother," she said, blowing smoke out her nose. "He's the holy do-gooder around here."

"Are you the one that bought the house...."

"You gotta be kiddin'. I didn't buy the house. My stupid sister did."

I froze, when Bea's eyes dared me to ask her one more question.

She stood a bit shorter than my five-foot-six, but heavier, looking like an unkempt brawler from a saloon on the wrong side of town. Considering her silver hair and weathered skin, I figured she was in her late fifties and still strong as a moose—not someone I wanted to tangle with.

Chapter 3

Tuesday morning, oh-dark-hundred, I woke up stiff and sore from Monday's work at the nursery. I remembered Bea telling me to go home, that Jason didn't like to pay overtime, and she would close up the place. I had no idea what closing up involved. How does one close a three-sided shack? Jason wasn't around, so I'd headed home to a hot bath and Campbell's chicken noodle soup for dinner. Solow approved the menu and received a splash of chicken broth on his kibble.

Preparing for another day at the nursery involved a book bag full of snacks, wool leggings and a botanical dictionary. But what I really needed was patience. Could I take another day of Bea? I dressed in Levis, two sweaters, leggings and rubber boots, topped off with the big green nursery jacket. I hoisted Solow into the passenger seat of my mud-spattered pickup. Even though the day was grey, the weatherman had promised sunshine in the afternoon.

It was just me and my dog cruising across the landscape, up the mountain, down the mountain, then left into the WildWest Nursery. It was already eight-fifteen.

Bea scowled at me like I was an hour late.

"I opened up the shop and put the coffee on. Now I'm on break," she exclaimed, as she dropped into her rattan chair under the 'No Smoking' sign.

Her first puff of attitude nauseated me.

"Bea, I'm allergic to smoke so I'll work in the warehouse for a while."

"Jason wants you to repot some hibiscus."

"Okay, where are they?" I said, as I quickly pulled my little dictionary out of the book bag, flipped the pages to "H" and silently read... "any of the large genus (Hibiscus) of herbs, shrubs, or small trees of the mallow family with dentate leaves and large showy flowers."

When I questioned Bea about the color of a "hibiscuits," she looked at me as if I just came from Mars and had never seen a plant before. Actually, I had seen plants all my life. I just never paid attention to them, except for Christmas trees and poison oak.

"Just point me to the hibiscuits and I'll repot them," I said jauntily, still not clear whether they were herbs, shrubs or small trees.

Following Bea was easy, as all her movements were slow.

"That's my heel ya stepped on," she crabbed.

"Sorry, I was looking for the hibiscuits...."

"Hibiscus," she said, in a loud husky voice.

A gust of wind shot across the valley floor, fluttering six acres of young plant leaves as it went. We stopped and zipped up our jackets. Next door, looking east, Sarah's eighteen-acre winery was covered in the skeletal remains of thousands of grape vines stretched across endless rows of wire fencing. Their leaves had turned from green to yellow to gone. Wineries striped the hills and flatland in every direction except to the West, where wooded mountains separated coastal towns and culture from the hustle-bustle of Gilroy and the Santa Clara Valley.

Bea walked up to a stack of empty five-gallon buckets and a waist-high mound of dirt.

"Okay, ya got yer dirt here and yer buckets there, and them's the biscuits yer lookin for." She pointed to a couple dozen plants, rolled her eyes and turned to leave.

Trying to ignore her snarkiness, I said, "By the way, Bea, what brought you to this line of work?"

"My brother needed an honest employee. He couldn't find one so he hired me," she laughed. "To tell ya the truth, I needed his help," she said as she walked off.

The repotting would have been simple if it hadn't been for the nasty root systems that clung tenaciously to the insides of the little pots like dandruff to a black sweater. The repotting was easy once the plants were yanked out of their comfort zone, but fifteen minutes later only two plants had been set free. I was so into my work that I didn't even notice Bea walking toward me with tools in her hands.

"These might help," she said, dropping a couple gardening implements on the ground.

"Thanks," I said, noticing that the sky had turned blue and the sun shone brightly. I slipped out of my green jacket and hung it on a post. My work became a tiny bit easier using the trowel and claw thingy. But I accidentally discovered that my foot worked the best. Feeling like the job would take all day, I stepped on a pot, maybe I even kicked it, which loosened the plant. I began stepping on all of the pots with glee. I even talked to the plants, promising a roomy new pot if they would just let go of the old one.

I wiped my brow with the back of my grubby hand and pulled off my cardigan sweater, wishing I could trade my rubber boots for a pair of sandals.

Laying into another stubborn potted plant, I said, "Get out of that pot, you dirty...."

"Hey, Jo, how's it going?" Jason laughed.

"Oh, hi, Jason, back from Fresno already?" I felt my cheeks redden as I let go of the muddy pot and straightened up.

"Yeah, I left at four this morning. Would you like to go have lunch with me?" He stared at my half-finished mess of plants, dirt and pots.

"Sure, I should be finished here in a few minutes."

"Yeah, with help," he laughed. Fifteen minutes later, all of the hibiscus had been transplanted, thanks to Jason's knowhow.

"So Bea is your sister?"

"My baby sister," he chuckled. "I'm glad you two are getting along. She's not the easiest person to get along with. Had some tough times in her life."

"Where is Fern in the family line-up?"

"She's the middle-child, nothing but trouble."

"I'm an only child. I wouldn't know about stuff like that."

He grinned. "I picked up a couple lunches from Erik's Deli. Thought we might have a picnic over at Sarah's Vineyard today."

"That sounds wonderful, but I'm afraid all I have to wear are these boots...."

"No problem, we'll eat outside at a picnic table. Not many people around on a weekday this time of year." He stacked the empty pots inside each other and we carried them back to the "bone yard," as Jason called the area behind the gift shop where stacks of black plastic pots waited their turn to be useful.

"What about Bea's lunch...?"

"She's on a special diet, all carbs, sodas and cigarettes. I gave her a nutritious sandwich from Erik's Deli. Hope she eats it," he said, his voice turning to a whisper.

We took turns washing our hands at one of the outdoor faucets, walked east along the edge of Hecker Pass Road and strolled up to the main building at Sarah's Vineyard. As we stepped into the lovely wine-tasting room full of dark wood and chrome, I noticed several people sitting at tables and a few at the bar. They were nicely dressed and none of them wore rubber boots.

"I feel out of place here," I whispered to Jason.

"Why? You're the prettiest woman here."

My caution buzzer instantly went off. Did I hear what I thought I heard? Jason knew all about my neighbor and fiancé, David Galaz, so why would he say a crazy thing like that?

"Thank you," I said, trying to be polite.

"Relax, I'm just picking up a couple of glasses and a bottle of wine," he whispered in my ear.

"I don't drink; it makes me crazy," I said.

"No problem. I'll take care of this bottle," Jason grinned.

His words did not pacify me. Still on alert, I let myself enjoy the sun, the smell of freshly cut lawn and a stunning view of ten million grapevines.

"This sandwich is delicious," I said.

"Yeah, they know how to make 'em all right. I heard you're a painter."

I swallowed the food in my mouth. "I paint murals."

"I was thinking of having something painted on the warehouse, you know, the long wall facing the parking lot. Something to make the place look inviting." He took a sip of wine. "Sure you wouldn't like to taste this wine?"

"If I taste the wine and mess up stuff at the nursery this afternoon, will you still pay me?"

"Really? You're that bad?" he laughed.

Actually, I had several unspoken reasons not to indulge. I would probably fall asleep on the job, I might say something to Bea that I would regret, and I didn't trust Jason's testosterone as far as I could toss him with one hand.

We finished our sandwiches and headed back to the nursery.

When we arrived at the gift shop, I thanked Jason for lunch and asked if he needed me to repot anything. He shook his head and told me to take over at the gift shop since the place was obviously empty. A half-eaten sandwich lay on the counter beside the cash register. A long cigarette lying on the concrete floor emitted wisps of smoke, and a can of soda pop lay on the floor draining into a puddle of brown liquid.

A gust of spooky-sounding wind batted ropes hanging from a flagpole just outside the gift shop.

"Where's Bea?" I gulped.

"That's what I'd like to know," Jason's voice cracked. "She's about as reliable as the Sunday mail."

"There's no Sun...oh, I see what you mean."

I worked in the gift shop the rest of the day while Jason talked to customers and made deliveries. I left work a little after five o'clock, and parked behind a Sheriff's cruiser in my driveway at about six. It was already dark. Two heads turned to look into my headlights, two doors opened and Sheriff Lund and her partner Sheriff Sayer walked to the front porch.

Fumbling for a house key, I caught up to my old acquaintances and led them into the house.

Solow gave a howling warm welcome, the one he would give to any old friend.

Sheriff Lund stood by the door with perfect posture and every blond hair pulled tight into a bun at the nape of her neck. She parted her thin, pale lips.

"Ms. Stuart, we have a few questions for you concerning the death of your neighbor, Mrs. Oeblick." Officer Lund pushed her thumbs into her holster belt.

"Please sit down," I said, waving my hand toward the old sofa.

"Thank you," Sheriff Sayer said, still carrying around a glint in his dark eyes and an easy-going grace in his dark-skinned body. I noticed his natty black hair had a lot more grey in it than a few months ago. I guessed that "sheriffing" was a pretty high-pressure job and might cause premature aging, or having Lund for a partner could do it too.

I sat in the rocker.

Lund pulled out a pad and pencil. "Ms. Stuart...."

"You can call me Josephine," I smiled nervously.

"Josephine, how well do you know Jason Oeblick?"

"Not very well, but he's a very nice employer. I work at his nursery."

"And how long have you been working there?" Sheriff Sayer asked.

"Two days."

"Only two days?" Lund said, her pencil hovering over the tablet.

"Yep, and Jason took me to lunch today at the winery next door." Oops, should I have said that? The last thing I wanted to do was make Jason look bad.

Lund scowled, and wrote something. Probably "hussy."

"Did you know his mother, Mrs. Oeblick?" she asked.

"No, I never met the poor lady, but I saw her walking her dog a few times. I heard that someone pushed her off her balcony."

"We can't confirm that information," Sheriff Lund said.

Sayer rubbed his chin. "We can tell you that Mrs. Oeblick was murdered, and we're looking for leads in this case. If you know anything, feel free to call us." He handed me his card. When they were gone, I filed it.

Chapter 4

Rain pounded the roof over my bedroom Wednesday morning causing me to scrunch further down under the blankets. My radio alarm continued to harass me with music from a local high school symphony orchestra. Duty nagged. I should rise, shine and work for Jason even though I didn't quite trust him. I didn't believe he killed his mother, but I did believe he was a lady-killer. Good looking for a sixty-year-old—strong, cheerful, full of manliness, and Jason had made a pass at me the day before. Or was that my imagination? And where did that flaky sister of his go?

Jason had told me he was going to interview a couple of people to help out at the nursery until Bea came back. I had suggested calling the police, but he told me not to worry, that she had flaked many times before.

Somehow the soda pop on the floor had touched a nerve in the back of my neck. I knew Bea was tactless, annoying and lazy, but a litterbug too?

As I showered, dressed and prepared myself for another day in the elements, it occurred to me that Solow would be happier with me than at home all alone and vice-versa. I fed him kibble and half of my breakfast, let him outside for a Fluffy chase and gathered up his water bowl and a long leash. I hoisted him into the passenger seat of my pickup, drove to Watsonville, turned onto Hecker Pass Road and arrived at the nursery before anyone else. The gravel parking lot was empty except for a green van and a matching delivery truck. A long eight-foot high sliding metal gate stretched across the front of the gift shop. A combination padlock held everything in place.

Peeking through the gate, I noticed that the soda mess had been cleaned up and the sandwich was gone from the counter. Solow howled, his nose pointing toward a trash can near the register.

"All that breakfast and you want an old beat up sandwich too?"

He gave me a sad-eyed look.

"Let's take a walk. You don't need any more food." I hooked the leash onto his collar and pulled him away from his fixation, Bea's rotting half sandwich in the trash. Walking east toward a puny winter sun, Solow led the way. His tail stretched upward, nose to the ground, ears dragging. As we walked along, I made a mental note of the pansies in the wheelbarrow and the rows of baby oak and pine trees. Almost everything else was foreign to me.

Solow pulled forward, aiming at the far end of the nursery property where a low wire fence ran between Sarah's Vineyard and the nursery. Against the fence stood a small wooden tool shed, weathered and alone.

Solow howled and pulled harder.

"Hey, quiet down old boy."

He howled again, long and hard as we approached the shed.

"What's your problem?"

Another howl.

He stopped at the shed. I opened the door, and Solow pushed past me into the dim interior.

Something moved.

Expecting to see a possum or a rat, I timidly peeked inside. It looked like Solow had found something interesting. When it moved again, I saw a yellow boot—just like the ones Bea wore.

Moving closer, I saw Bea's matted grey hair and her bulky body curled up in front of the shovels and rakes hanging on the wall. I bent down and touched her hand. It felt cool, but not cold.

Solow licked Bea's face until she opened her eyes and shouted at him to stop.

My heart bounced with joy. The woman was alive. I gave Bea a hand, tugging at her until she was standing. She tilted this way and that, but finally steadied herself. When we stepped outside into daylight, I looked her over. Mangled spider webs clung to her jeans and her jacket, and something black crawled over the top of her head.

Instinctively I swatted at it with my hand.

"Ouch! Whatcha think yer doin'?" she snarled.

"I just swatted a spider off your head...."

Bea felt the top of her head. Tears welled. "It bit me, I know it bit me."

"Take it easy. I flicked it away before it could bite you." Was she really that scared of a stupid spider? At least she was capable of being emotional. Maybe she was human after all.

"So, Bea, how did you end up in the shed?" I asked, trying not to look like I was butting into her business.

"I musta sleep-walked. I do that sometimes," she said, turning at the sound of Jason's pickup truck crunching gravel as it pulled to a stop in front of the gift shop. "We better get back," she said, walking ahead of me across many acres of potted greenery.

Solow and I stayed close behind Bea in case she teetered too far to one side and fell over. A few yards from the shop, I veered off the path and walked up to a row of straggly looking young trees in ten-inch pots. The labels said they were 'Sempervirens,' but they looked like Charlie Brown Christmas trees to me. Another row of similar trees were labeled, 'Redwoods.' So much to remember, but I was determined to learn as much about plants and trees as possible.

To my chagrin, Solow marked a Charlie Brown tree.

When Jason had had enough time to calm Bea down and roll the gate open, I walked into the shop. Various blooming plants had already been set out in a wheelbarrow display. Bea sat in her usual chair puffing her usual cigarette with her usual can of soda at the ready.

Jason opened the till to count the money, but there wasn't any to count. He looked at Bea. "What happened to all the money?"

"How do I know, I was in the shed, remember?"

"He was here, wasn't he?" Jason asked in a restrained voice, probably because I entered the room. It felt like a family battle, so I slipped back outside where I could still hear but not be seen. I bent down to read the label on a pretty little potted plant adorned with several rusty-red flowers. I recognized it from similar plants in my mother's back yard garden. The label read "Chrysanthemum."

My mom grew roses. She even belonged to the Rose Club. What a disappointment I must have been, not knowing a bulb from a broom.

Jason rounded the corner of the shop looking as one might look after a ten-hour-day of hard labor, but it was only nine-thirty in the morning.

"Everything okay, Jason?"

"Sure…Josephine," he laughed. "You're lucky you don't have any brothers or sisters."

"Maybe, but I've often wished I did. But I'm lucky I still have Mom and Dad, and they're healthy and active. Actually, that's putting it mildly. They're coming up on eighty, and they act half their age—boating, dancing, skating, camping, hiking and Dad still bowls."

"That's great," Jason said, his eyes focused on his feet. "I miss my mom, and my dad spends all day in a wheelchair. I think his mind is going."

"That's too bad. What's your other sister like?" I asked.

"Fern has a lot of energy. Did I mention that we're all adopted?"

"No," I said, but the idea had crossed my mind. That would explain Bea's darker complexion, brown eyes and thicker build.

"And there's my brother, Rico. They got him on a trip to Rio de Janeiro. He was ten years old. Here it is forty years later, and he still sounds like a Portagee," Jason laughed.

"How did your folks manage to adopt him?"

"Ever hear of human trafficking? My dad is a wheeler-dealer kinda guy. He had money. Always got what he wanted—including my wife." Jason turned and walked back to the gift shop. His bitterness followed him like a cold dark shadow.

I read a few more plant labels, most of them written in gobbledygook—Latin maybe. Like the marigold, known as *tagetes erecta*, an annual in the *asteraceae* family, and the daylily, known as *hemerocallis* hybrid, a perennial in the *liliaceae* family. Who knew—certainly not me!

Since I already knew that the plant names would dissolve quickly in my brain, I gave up and marched back to the shop to find out what my day's work would be. As I turned to go inside, I smacked into Jason coming the other way carrying a tall stack of empty black plastic pots.

"Sorry, Josephine, I need you to repot the day lilies."

"No problem," I smiled. Fortunately, I knew exactly where the lilies were because I had just been there. Maybe I could get a grip on this horticulture stuff after all. With great confidence, I unpotted thirty little root-bound lilies and repotted them in eight-inch pots. I was so engrossed in my work that when I finally looked around, I realized there were several customers wandering the grounds.

I noticed that the company delivery truck was missing.

As I stood up and brushed dirt off my Levis with filthy hands, a tall slim woman wearing her red hair short and straight, approached me asking for a thirty-pound sack of chicken manure.

Solow sniffed the woman's hand-knit multi-colored angora socks.

We walked to the gift shop and found Bea asleep in her chair.

"Bea," I said, tapping her shoulder.

"Now what do ya want?" She looked up and saw the customer.

"This lady is looking for a thirty-pound sack of chicken manure," I said, smiling politely while discreetly gnashing my teeth.

"That ain't no lady!" Bea shouted.

"And you are not a bee, you silly goose. I didn't know you were working for Jason." By that time, they were in a serious hug.

I scratched my head. Did they like each other or were they attacking each other?

"Josephine, this here's mah sister, Fern," Bea bellowed.

"Wow, I guess the only one missing is Rico…." I said.

The room went silent.

"How do you know about him?" Bea glared at me.

Fern's green-eyed stare was just as deadly.

"Jason and I were just talking about our families," I said, thinking how dissimilar the sisters were. Bea squat and lazy with tons of grey hair as compared to Fern's tall skinny frame, light coloring and stringy red hair.

The women turned their backs to me and walked past the restrooms to the big storage barn. A minute later, Fern came back with a sack of chicken manure slung over her shoulder. She turned to Bea, said goodbye and walked out to her shiny black Mercedes.

I didn't see any money exchanged.

"Where did Jason go?" I asked Bea.

"Well, if it's any of yer business, he's deliverin' some palm trees and goin' to the bank." She plopped down in her chair and lit a cigarette.

"I'll go help customers," I said, yearning for fresh air and new people with questions. I had discovered that I actually enjoyed helping people. It was a fifty-fifty proposition. Half the time I was helping them, and half the time they were telling me the names of plants and where and how to grow them.

One o'clock sharp the taco truck arrived. Bea was first in line. They took our orders and on the way out, the taco truck squeezed by Jason's truck as he returned from his delivery. He parked, climbed out and sadly watched the food truck merge into traffic.

"Jason," I said, walking up to him, "I bought you a burrito."

"Thanks, Jo, I'm starving." He took the burrito and walked into the shop.

I ate my lunch sitting on an old wrought iron bench backed up to the outside eastern wall of the gift shop with Solow at my feet. Unfortunately, the sun was shining on the opposite side of the building where there was nothing to sit on. I pulled my phone out of my jacket pocket and punched Alicia's number.

"Jo, I was wondering when I'd hear from you. How's it going?"

"Not as bad as the first day. I like the work and I'm learning so much. The only hard part is a certain employee with a bad attitude. Other than that, I'm good. Jason said he might have me paint a mural on one side of the big building where they keep tools and sacks of stuff like manure. It depends on whether he can find someone to take my place."

"There must be a labor shortage these days," she snickered.

"So, there's this mystery going on around here...."

"Here we go again," Alicia chuckled.

"Really, Allie, something's going on. Solow and I found Bea, Jason's sister, in the tool shed this morning. She'd been there all night."

"That's weird."

"The weirdest part was when she told me how it happened. She said she'd been sleepwalking. Can you believe it?"

"No, she's just blowing you off. You better be careful, Jo, the next thing you'll find will be a guy named Jack climbing a bean stalk."

My next call was to David, who had the same type of reaction to my "Bea story" as Alicia's.

I didn't bother calling Mom since she usually lived in the same camp as Alicia and David. The "I don't believe it camp."

Even my dreams that night were against me. Instead of dreaming about a man named Jack climbing a bean stalk, I dreamt that I discovered a very old man wearing white whiskers and red long johns climbing the flag pole outside the nursery. I asked the man if he wanted to buy a plant. He didn't answer, but he did drop an empty clay pot on my head. In my dream, David found me the next day lying in the tool shed, and scolded me for not being more careful.

Chapter 5

It was Thursday and once again, Solow and I were headed east on Highway 152, over Hecker Pass into the rising sun and WildWest Nursery, where the unusual had become usual. Solow tagged along as I opened the rolling gate and fired up the little electric wall heater in the open-air gift shop. Even on the highest setting, I had to stand close to feel the warmth. Six feet away, the cash register was frozen shut.

Solow and I trudged out to the shed at the far end of the property to make sure Bea wasn't in it. She wasn't. As we walked among the long rows of potted vegetation, crisp frosty air gave way to a sunny day promising to be in the low sixties. My big green company jacket proved to be too warm and my jeans/sweatshirt outfit, not quite warm enough. But Solow was comfortable bouncing along the path wearing nothing but his birthday suit.

Jason's black pickup truck pulled to a stop in front of the gift shop.

Solow greeted him with a friendly howl.

"Hi Jason, is Bea coming in today?"

"No, not today, I've hired two new people. I was hoping to replace you...."

"Oh, I'm sorry I didn't...."

"No, no, your work is fine, Josephine. But I want you to paint a mural right here on this wall facing the parking lot," he said, waving his hand at the old stucco warehouse wall, all twenty-five feet of it.

Instantly my mind ran through at least ten theme ideas, everything from an elaborate trompe l'oeil (fool the eye) building to a pond full of bull frogs and lily pads.

The stream of ideas stopped abruptly when a rusty red pickup rolled across the parking lot, stopping just short of Jason's foot. Solow sniffed the tires and decided he liked the smell of old equipment. He sniffed the gal climbing out of the truck and seemed to like her boots.

She walked up to Jason.

"Hi, boss, we're ready to start." The young woman smiled. She looked at me. "Hi, my name is Caitlin."

As Caitlin and I shook hands, I noticed her pale skin, freckles and blue eyes. Something about her didn't make sense. Inconsistent with her fair Irish looks, a long black braid of hair hung over one shoulder. She flipped it back with a toss of her head.

As we talked, a teenage boy climbed out of the passenger seat, one ear plugged into his cell phone. Caitlin reached out and pulled the cord from his right ear.

"Sorry, I forgot it was there," he said, quickly tucking his phone into a pocket. "I'm Lito," he smiled, standing a foot taller than his mom. The only resemblance between them was the sparkly blue eyes. He had smooth light brown skin and thick black hair due for a haircut.

While Jason walked the newcomers into the gift shop, and showed them around the property, I studied the ten-foot-high stucco wall, conjuring up a few more mural ideas.

When Jason finally came back to the parking lot, he pulled an old photo out of his shirt pocket and handed it to me.

"Does this mean you want me to paint a bucking horse…?" I asked.

"Yep, with me on it—younger, of course," he laughed.

"What about the rest of the wall?"

"Josephine, you're the artist. I'm sure you'll come up with something."

"The wall needs a fresh coat of paint...."

"I have some white paint that you and Lito can use." Jason turned and walked away.

Leaving Solow asleep in the sun, I shuffled over to the gift shop, and turned the corner to go inside. Jason bustled by me carrying a gallon of paint in each hand. I followed him out to "the wall" where he left the paint.

"I'll get a ladder and some brushes," he said over his shoulder as he headed back for more stuff. I followed Jason through the shop, into the warehouse where we gathered up tarps and paint rollers and such.

In the far corner of the building, Lito was organizing a row of bins with all sizes of pruners and clippers. As we were leaving, he grabbed an eight-foot ladder and followed us out to "the wall."

Jason put the ladder in position. "Okay, you two, your work for today is to paint this wall white. I'll be leaving for Santa Cruz with a full load of maples as soon as I get them loaded."

Lito and I looked at each other.

"I'll paint the top...."

"That's very kind of you, Lito. I'll paint the bottom half." Silently I wondered if he volunteered to do the ladder work because of my age? As it turned out, we worked well together.

"My mom says you live down the road from us," Lito said, not missing a stroke with the roller.

"I didn't know you lived on Otis."

"Yeah, we moved into Jason's cottage a couple of months ago. I'm glad he finally got Mom to work for him. Her last job had crazy hours."

"What about you? Aren't you supposed to be in school?"

"I graduated in June. Skipped a grade," he chuckled.

"That's wonderful; now what are you going to do?" I asked, looking up. A glob of paint splatted on my boot. "Darn it, I'll be right back."

Bam, I ran into Jason. "Sorry—paint." I pointed to my left foot and kept going. Luckily, I was able to wash the paint off my boot before it dried. When I got back to the job, Jason's delivery truck was gone, and Lito had finished the top portion of the wall. He helped me roll on the bottom half and cleaned up the mess. Not only did he take orders, he was a self-starter. Wherever Lito saw work to be done, he figured out how to do it and did it.

His mom, on the other hand, had been instructed to load eight geraniums in ten-inch pots into the van so I could deliver them to a winery two miles down the road. I peeked into the back of the van.

Caitlin started to close the doors.

"Hold it," I said, re-counting the geraniums. "I think they wanted eight plants in ten-inch pots."

"Oh dear!" Caitlin slapped her forehead. "Those are eight-inch pots." She quickly loaded them onto a flat bed cart and came back with eight lovely geraniums in ten-inch pots. "Thanks, Josephine," she said.

"No problem—been there, done that." I fired up the van and made a quick trip to the designated winery, thinking about what Jason had told me earlier. He said that Sarah's Vineyard bought ten potted bamboo plants for their patio last week and now the competition, Four Oaks Vineyard, had ordered red geraniums to spruce up their patio. That kind of competition could only be good for Jason's business.

After a quick late lunch break, Caitlin and I raked the paths and helped customers wandering the property while Lito waited on people in the gift shop. An hour later, Jason returned and told me to go home early so I could prepare for painting the mural the next day.

"But you don't even know how much I charge...."

"I know the mural will be excellent. I've already asked around about you, and I know you're a reasonable person. Did I tell you I want a WildWest sign as part of the mural?"

"Okay, that's doable," I frowned.

"What's the matter, Josephine?"

"I hate sign painting, but I'll do it."

Lito stepped closer and whispered in my ear, "I'm a very good sign painter."

Jason's last words were, "Let Lito help you so we can get this done before it rains again."

It sounded to me like no matter how bad Lito's painting might be, it would be okay with Jason.

I decided to go say goodbye to Caitlin, who was raking the far corner of the property.

"Caitlin, I didn't know you lived on Jason's property."

Suddenly her cheeks went pink. She gazed at me as if I were an eavesdropper, someone not minding her own business.

"Lito said you're renting the cottage."

"Yes, we are but please don't repeat that information. Let's just say, someone might be looking for us and we don't want to be found."

"Oh, sorry. I'm curious about Mrs. Oeblick's death—thought you would know more about it, that's all."

Her cheeks went from pink to red. "We weren't home that day." She turned and began raking again.

"Do you happen to know where Jason's father lives?"

She shook her head and raked with faster, harder strokes.

Confident that Caitlin and her teenage son could handle the nursery business without me, I hefted Solow into the truck and drove home with visions of a WildWest mural in my head. I figured I could finish the job in ten days with Lito's help. Hopefully, the weather would work in our favor. But if we had to take some time off for rain, I thought I would still finish in time to start the Gilroy Library mural at the end of the month.

Trucking up Otis Road, knowing that Jason was working at the nursery, I decided to check on his property. It was the neighborly thing to do. We rolled past David's house and mine, Solow sniffing the air as usual, on up to the Oeblick place. I was surprised to see a white van with a ladder strapped to the roof, parked in the driveway. I figured someone was delivering something, or fixing something. I saw an older guy wearing a Giants baseball cap sitting in the driver's seat. He looked at me, fired up the van and left.

Feeling a bit curious, I walked up to the front door to see if a package had been delivered. All I found was an envelope pushed into the crack under the door. I gently pulled it free and noticed the flap was tucked, not sealed. I hesitated, looked at Solow's head and shoulders hanging out the truck window, and decided I should make sure the envelope didn't contain something that would harm Jason, considering his mother had recently been murdered.

A gust of wind hit the back of my neck and rustled clumps of red and gold leaves still clinging to a tall maple tree next to the driveway. My new horticulture awareness was paying off—I knew the difference between an oak tree and a maple. I had the feeling someone was watching me, but saw no one. Across the street, a pair of drapes closed.

The envelope flapped in the wind, escaping my grip. It headed up toward a bay window and then took a dive straight down into a large rose bush. I walked up to the bush, leaned in and snagged my sleeve on several thorns.

"Good grief, how do I get loose?" I mumbled to myself. The more I fought, the more stuck I became.

Solow barked encouragingly.

Every time I pulled away from a thorn, another one caught my arm. I couldn't leave the envelope in the bush—what if it was important? While one arm was stuck to the bush, I reached in with the other arm, grabbed the envelope and tried to pull back. With both arms stuck in the bush and Solow snickering—I mean whimpering behind my back—I was close to tears.

A vehicle drove up and a car door slammed.

Great! I couldn't even turn my head far enough to see who was coming. Was it Mrs. Oeblick's murderer?

"Need some help?" a manly voice asked.

"Oh, David, get me out of this bush!" I cried.

"Hang on, honey, I'll work you loose." He pulled out a pocketknife and began cutting the offending little branches. When he finished, I was free of the bush but several nasty sprigs were still attached to my jacket sleeves.

"How did you find me...?" I asked.

"I was headed over to your house, but you pulled out and headed up the road so I followed you up here."

"Good. I'll see you at my house," I said, just before he kissed my cheek.

"What's that in your hand, Josie?"

My face suddenly felt hot. "I was leaving a note for Jason...about work...he wants me to paint a mural at the nursery, but the wind got it and it landed in the bush. Thanks for rescuing me. I don't know what I would have done without you."

"Just another damsel in distress," he laughed.

"I'll meet you at my house, okay?"

"No problem," he said, and drove away, leaving me alone with the envelope. I opened it, and read: "I think I know who killed your mother. Call me."

The note ended with an illegible signature. "The man must be a doctor," I said to Solow.

Chapter 6

Friday morning, the end of my workweek was at hand, and Jason expected preliminary sketches for his mural. I had spent ninety percent of Thursday evening sketching and packing up my paints and equipment. Ten percent of my time was spent with David. He went home right after dinner when it became obvious that all I could think about was preparing for the new mural job. As a muralist, I had already painted dozens and dozens of murals, large and small; but historically, each new project had sent me into a temporary tizzy. Fortunately, I discovered that large doses of chocolate ice cream helped my nervous condition.

More than happy to be going somewhere, Solow waited beside the truck for help getting into his seat. I told him if he gained one more pound, he would have to climb in on his own. Sitting side-by-side with my buddy, I paused to remember if I had packed everything: the sketches, level, chalk, short and medium ladders, brushes, rags, paint, masking tape, empty containers and so on. Dressed in a fat jacket, leg warmers, boots, knitted cap and open-finger gloves, I thought I was ready for any eventuality.

Knowing how excited I was about the new job, David arrived to see me off. "Josie, you look like you're trying out for best-dressed snow bunny."

"Oh, thanks a lot," I laughed, knowing how ridiculous I looked in my mismatched cold-weather paint-gear, but feeling confident I would be comfortably warm working outdoors in the November chill. He kissed me and whispered something sweet in my ear. Why did he have to be such a good sport? But the job beckoned and I was excited.

Solow and I had a merry time gobbling up the miles, singing to the radio and enjoying warmth from the heater. When I finally realized the cab was getting hot, I shut off the heater. But the heat kept coming—maybe it was a hot-flash. I yanked off my cap and gloves, rolled down the window and finally pulled to the side of the road so that I could take off my boots, allowing me to slide the leg warmers off. Twisted down into a knot, better known as the yoga pretzel pose, I looked up and Solow licked the sweat running down my cheek.

"Thanks, sweetie, love you too.

Something big and boxy whipped by, shaking my little Mazda like a Chihuahua in the jaws of a German Shepherd.

Someone honked—my head hit the steering wheel. I tried to straighten up in my seat, but my back refused to cooperate. I took a breath. Slowly, gently, I began pulling myself up, one vertebra at a time.

"Okay, I can do this," I told Solow.

He yawned and curled up in his seat. I think he rolled his eyes.

Sitting up straight and back in control, I fired up the truck and we pressed on, up and over Hecker Pass with its chain of hairpin turns followed by the downhill, lovely forested eastern slope. So much beauty on one mountain, plus the occasional crack-up like the one up ahead. I braked. Recognizing an off-white Nissan hatchback wearing multiple stickers disseminating saintly advice, I pulled the truck to a stop in front of the vehicle.

My lower back let me know it wasn't happy, as I climbed out of my truck.

Bea rose up into view beside the Nissan's right front tire.

"Josephine, give me a hand," she demanded.

My first thought was, "Why should I?" but I followed directions and helped her rip the front bumper off the frame, allowing the wheels to turn.

"What happened to your car, Bea?"

"Dang Bronco slowed for a curve. My brakes ain't so good and I ran up his backside. Not a scratch on the Bronco, but my bumper is shot. Course it wasn't too good to start with...." she grunted, as we carried the flimsy bumper to the back of the car and tossed it into the crowded trunk already half filled with boxes of old clothes and household items.

"Going to the Good Thrift Store?" I asked.

"No, I ain't goin' to the Good Thrift," she snarked. "I'm dumpin' this junk off at my dad's place. It was Mom's stuff and he can deal with it now."

"I'll help you drop it off...." I said.

"Ain't you the nosey one? I packed and loaded that junk myself, I'll unload it myself."

I said goodbye to Ms. Grump and headed down the mountain, not even looking back to see if her car was in basic running condition. A couple of miles later, I noticed her car was right behind me.

I took the left turn into the WildWest parking lot and stopped next to Caitlin's pickup. She and Lito had just arrived and were clambering out of their seats.

Looking around, I realized that Bea had continued down the road toward Gilroy. Jason had already rolled back the gift shop gate. I spotted him pulling a flatbed cart loaded with flowering bushes of some sort. His breath floated in the cold air as he trudged toward the company delivery truck. On his way, he stopped in front of the shop, glanced at the folder I was carrying and smiled.

"Josephine, can I see the sketches?"

"Sure, let's sit in front of the heater."

If Bea decided to come to work, I wasn't about to let the ungrateful woman have her favorite chair in front of the only heat on the property. We entered the shop, Jason placed a stool next to Bea's chair and we sat down. I opened the folder.

"One picture?" he said, looking puzzled.

"Just one. Sometimes I have a hard time deciding what to paint, but this time it was easy. I apologize for the rough sketch—it's more for placement than anything. We start with the golden Gilroy hills in the background and a sprinkling of oak trees. Moving forward we have patches of green grass, a bigger oak and some poppies over here and a few cows grazing over there. Moving forward, we have the bucking horse with you on it and in front of that we have a rustic wooden fence."

"You're right, Josephine, there's only one way to do this painting and you nailed it. But lose the fence." His grin let me know he was excited about the project, and I was happy to not paint a fence.

"All I need now are some close-up pictures of the hardware on the horse," I said. "I don't know a lot about bridles and such and don't want to get it wrong."

"What about the WildWest sign?" he scratched his chin.

"That goes across the top. Lito has already volunteered to paint it. I brought my paints and I'm ready to start."

Jason held up his hands and laughed, "I couldn't stop you if I tried."

Lito stood against the wall next to the boss listening to our plans, his eyes glued to the sketch. He followed me outside and helped unload the truck and set up the ladders. I explained that painting the sky would be the first order of business. After that, I would paint hills and a meadow while Lito penciled and then painted the WildWest signage across the sky.

Jason loaded the last of the foliage into his delivery truck and drove away.

Lito helped me carry ladders, paint and tools over to Jason's eight-foot ladder resting against the freshly painted wall. Using a level, I drew a horizon line, end-to-end, six feet up from the ground, which would give us four feet by twenty-five feet of sky. I poured white paint into a bucket of blue, and Lito stirred. I poured half of the new lighter blue paint into another container, added more white, and Lito stirred. I poured half of the lightest blue into a bucket, added more white plus a small amount of yellow paint, and Lito stirred.

"Hey, Josephine, I'm goin' stir-crazy," he laughed.

"This is how we make sky," I said, brushing a sample of each color onto a piece of white cardboard. I waved the samples in the air for a minute, since the true color wouldn't show until the paint was dry. "We have four good blues. Now we paint."

While standing four rungs up the six-foot aluminum ladder, Lito painted the top one-foot by twenty-five-foot stretch of stucco with the original and darkest of the three blues. I came along behind him on the five-foot ladder painting a one-foot stretch using medium blue, blending it into the first color as I went. When Lito finished the top portion, he stood on the ground, painting and blending one foot by twenty-five feet of the next lightest blue. I added a foot of the lightest blue, ending it at the horizon line. Lito was a quick study, and together we had created a beautiful four-foot by twenty-five-foot chunk of sky.

"I missed a spot," Lito said, pointing to a tiny bit of white showing through the blue near the top. He quickly scooted a ladder into position and carried his container of paint and a brush up four steps. With one quick stroke, the white spot disappeared.

A bee buzzed around Lito's head. He started to back down the ladder, juggling the paint and brush in one hand, holding onto the ladder with the other hand.

Suddenly several more bees joined the first one.

Lito dropped the paint can as he tried to swat bees away from his face.

Helplessly I watched as his right leg slipped off the rung.

A dozen bees attacked one side of his head.

Lito twisted and flailed his arm in the air...then two arms. His other foot slipped and pointed toward the sun as he dropped, butt first, onto a concrete berm positioned near the wall to keep cars from parking too close. He rolled off the berm and laid on his side, curled in a ball, tears filling his eyes. Red-faced, he finally let out a long pathetic moan.

Solow joined in with a long howl, obviously feeling Lito's pain.

Tears came to my eyes when Lito tried to stand up.

By that time, Caitlin was at his side, gently pulling him up.

"Oh my God...they stung your ear," she said. "Four, five stings on the ear, and two on your neck!" She flicked a dead bee off his shoulder.

"Never mind the ear, my butt is killing me," he groaned.

Caitlin and I walked Lito into the gift shop, but he refused to sit in the chair. His mother finally called their doctor who was solidly booked, but gave them his lunch hour when he heard Lito's groans. It was eleven-thirty when Caitlin fired up her pickup with Lito lying on his stomach in the truck bed with a blue plastic tarp wrapped around his shivering body.

That was the end of painting for me. As the only employee around, I needed to do nursery work. I handled all kinds of customers with a variety of questions and problems. My usual answer to them was, "Jason will be back soon." But he wasn't back, so I did the best I could. One lady asked for violets. I talked her into pansies. A man asked me for a box of snail bait. I couldn't find any so I told him to go to the local SPCA and adopt a duck. He seemed happy with the advice. I was on a roll. Another customer wanted to buy a weed whacker. She specified that it must be lightweight and easy for her to handle. I suggested she adopt a couple goats. She looked at me with distain and walked off.

Glad to see Ms. Weed Whacker peel out of the parking lot, I turned away from the sun. A large delivery truck painted deep blue rolled to a stop. The driver jumped down from his seat and handed me papers on a clipboard. I signed the paperwork for three palm trees. The middle-aged driver wore a white dress shirt and black tie to match his black slacks and shiny shoes. His sleek black hair was pulled into a man-bun. He scribbled his name under mine and gave me the pink copy.

The delivery man watched the irritable weed whacker woman storm into highway traffic and shook his head. "What's the matter with her?"

"She wanted a weed whacker, and I suggested she get a couple goats."

He shrugged his broad shoulders. "Works for me. Where's the old lady?" His dark eyes darted from the gift shop over to the shed and around to the front entrance gate.

"Bea isn't here today...."

"No," he softened his voice, "I meant the old lady, Mrs. Oeblick. She was knitting some stuff for me. Ah, a knitted cap." He grinned a grin that made him look somewhere between a Siamese cat and a politician.

"Didn't you hear? She was murdered." I saw exaggerated shock and disbelief wash across his pockmarked face.

"Jeez, I didn't know. I work out of LA, and I don't get up here very often. I was really hoping to pick up that, ah, knitting stuff I ordered," he said, as he opened the back of the truck and began off-loading three little palms trees.

"Are you sure she didn't leave a package for me?" he asked.

"I wouldn't know. You'd have to ask Jason, but he's not here right now. Who shall I say is asking?"

The man climbed into his shiny blue truck. "Ted."

"Who would want to kill a nice old lady?" I mused.

He looked down at me. "What makes you think she was nice?"

I watched Ted angle his truck through the open entrance gate and drive away, wondering why he had said such a negative thing about an old lady who knits things for him. But there was no time to contemplate such things. Customers kept coming and between customers, I carted one palm tree at a time over to the tropical tree section of the property. After all that, I raked leaves and prayed Lito would be all right, all the time wishing I was working on the new mural.

Hours later, when Caitlin came back to the nursery she was alone.

"Where's Lito?" I asked.

"I took him home. The doctor said he should lie on his stomach with ice on the tailbone. It's not broken, but it is badly bruised. He said it would take up to three weeks to heal."

"Oh, that's awful," I said, realizing for the first time that I'd have to paint the WildWest sign, unless.... A minute later, I was on the phone with Alicia. Without being too bossy, I persuaded her to come to work for me at the nursery. I figured just being in the company of thousands of plants, Alicia would be happy and in her element. And we could go to Sarah's Winery for a picnic lunch. And maybe she would do some sign painting.

My stomach growled.

Overly excited about painting at the nursery, I had neglected to think ahead and pack a lunch. And unable to leave the nursery, since I was the only employee around, I was running on empty in the food department.

I felt sorry for Caitlin, having an injured son to take care of, but figured nursery work would take her mind off of Lito's misery. Even though she looked rattled, I had to put the poor lady in charge of the place because Jason hadn't returned. I hoisted Solow into the truck, and we took off for Gilroy and the first fast food place I could find. Anything would do.

Chapter 7

Early on, Jason had informed me that WildWest Nursery did its best business on weekends. But I let him know that I was unavailable on Saturdays and Sundays. My priority was laundry, housework and a social life that included David and my folks.

Okay, it was Saturday afternoon and I hadn't even thought about housework. Why spoil a good weekend?

That morning I had sauntered down my long drive-way, wearing robe and slippers and collected three newspapers and three days worth of mail. Turning to walk back to the house, I heard the roar of an engine coming down the road toward town. Caitlin beeped her horn and whizzed by. It occurred to me that poor Lito might be home alone. Maybe I could go there and as-sess the situation.

After a lovely shower and a good breakfast, Solow and I were ready for a walk up Otis Road, a one-lane stretch of curves accommodating a couple dozen hous-es, each one standing on five acres. One side of the road was more woodsy than my side, where grassy hills had just a sprinkling of oak trees. Behind the homes on my side of the road, a stretch of eucalyptus trees paraded along the crest of hills, all the way from David's house to Jason's and beyond.

My mind was so busy, I barely noticed the chill in the air, turkey buzzards circling overhead, and the smell of dead skunk.

Solow bounced along on four short legs, happy to be going somewhere.

My cell phone rang.

"Good grief!" I said, pulling the little tyrant from my Levis pocket.

"Hi, Mom."

"It's not your mother. I'm using her phone while she's out...."

"Oh, hi, Dad, what's going on?" I stopped walking as cold wind hit my face.

Solow kept going, looking like a long-eared, long-bodied dog on short springs. I watched his bouncy rear end disappear around the bend. As I tried to catch up to him, Dad reminded me that Mom's surprise birthday party would begin in seven short hours, and I had volunteered to bring the cake.

"You're bringing the cake, aren't you?"

Fumbling to zip my jacket against the cold air, I dropped the phone on the road twice.

"Sure, Dad, and seventy-nine candles." But even as I said that, I was considering my options. Could I order a cake on such short notice? Did I have time to bake one myself? David was good at everything—should I ask him to bake a cake?

Dad's voice broke into my concentration. "Jo, are you there...?"

"I'm here, and it's getting windy. What time do you need the cake?"

"I was hoping to have it this afternoon. Leola's coming home from Aunt Clara's around six. I told everyone to be here at five-thirty, remember?"

We had arrived at Jason's property. With Dad on the line, I stood beside Jason's mailbox, my eyes searching the grounds for Solow. Nosy neighbor behind her drapes across the street to my right, and Solow sniffing the far side of half an acre of rich green lawn needing a mow in front of Jason's place. The grass was up to his thighs as he sniffed his way back to the driveway and up three wide stairs to Jason's front door.

"To tell you the truth, Dad, I've had a lot on my mind lately so I'm glad you called. Love you, bye."

I looked around the neighborhood. Curtains moved in the front window of the house across the street from Jason. I shoved the phone into my pocket, marched up to Jason's house and ignored the nosy neighbor.

Joining Solow at the front door, I rang the doorbell. Rang it again. The coast was clear—nobody home. We circled around the side of the house, ending at another front door, Caitlin and Lito's cottage door.

Imagining Lito lying on his belly, fast asleep in his bed, I tapped lightly on the door and let myself and Solow in. Lito stared at me from the couch, his hair stuck to one side of his head, blue eyes blurry, bare feet hanging over the end of the shabby piece of furniture.

"Hey, Lito, how's it goin?"

"Not real well—sorry I can't paint the sign...."

"Don't worry about it. My friend, Alicia is going to do it. I have something I want to try out on you."

He cringed. "I'm okay, really...."

"This is the best mixture of essential oils for pain," I said, pulling a small vial out of my pocket. I showed him the little roller under the cap. "I'm going to roll a couple drops on the bottom of each foot."

I dabbed at one foot.

Lito shrieked as his foot shot upward. His shrieks turned into giggles as I dabbed oil on the second foot. Tears streamed down his cheeks.

"Are you okay, Lito?"

"I'm very ticklish. I'll be all right...wow, I think I'm already doin' good, pain-wise." His mouth gaped. He was obviously considering the odds that the oil actually worked as a painkiller—an instant painkiller. I had used the stuff once when I rose up and bumped my head on the doorframe of my metal shed in the back yard. I too had been skeptical until I tried it.

"So, Lito, were you home the day Mrs. Oeblick was killed?"

"Ah, yeah. Why?"

"Just curious. Did you see anything unusual?"

"No, Josephine, I didn't. I'm really hungry...."

"No problem. I'll make a sandwich. What kind do you want?"

"We have peanut butter."

"Peanut butter is good," I said cheerfully, as I hunted for bread. I found a loaf next to the toaster, the one and only electrical appliance in the little kitchen. Luckily, one of the two food items in the fridge was a carton of milk. Two chairs and two folded TV trays had been pushed against the kitchen wall. I set up one of the trays on the carpet near Lito's head. Then came milk and a sandwich.

"Was that thunder I just heard?"

Lito didn't answer.

I had a strong urge to run home and take care of cake business.

"Thank you, Josephine," he said after the first bite.

"Do you need anything else before I leave?"

He vigorously shook his head no.

I was free to go, but I thought of one more question.

"The day Mrs. Oeblick was murdered and you didn't see anything...did you hear anything unusual?"

He stopped chewing. "I heard a car drive up in the afternoon, but I was reading and didn't bother to look outside. That reminds me, I sure would like to have something to read."

Lito pointed to the bathroom door. Sure enough, inside the tiny room, on the counter top was his *Mechanics Illustrated* magazine. As I crossed the front room and handed it to him, I noticed there was no TV, there were no comfy chairs or side tables. The bathroom had just one towel, a bar of soap, a bottle of black hair dye and a razor.

"Lito, maybe you'd be more comfortable in your bed...."

"This is my bed. Mom offered her bed but it's just a mattress on the floor, and it's too hard for me to get up and down with a sore butt."

Funny how guys roll with the punches, while a girl in that shabby situation would have been completely embarrassed if not devastated. I gave Lito one of my business cards in case he needed to call me for anything or remembered more about Mrs. Oeblick's last day on earth.

After a quick goodbye, my faithful companion and I trotted down Otis as fast as our legs would take us, my mind bouncing from one possible cake solution to another.

Solow followed me past our house another hundred yards to the ranch style house next door. David's little Miata was parked next to a late model silver Mercedes, like the one his dentist drove. I needed to see David, but I dreaded seeing Ms. Perfect Dentist, perfect hair, perfect everything. He didn't see anything wrong with perfection. Men are just clueless! Everyone knows that it's a woman's imperfections that are most endearing. But maybe David didn't read that article.

As these thoughts ran through my mind, the front door opened and Ms. Dentist said hello and walked down the path toward her car, a red purse slung over one shoulder to match her red heels.

David was right behind her.

Solow finally caught up to me and charged forth when he saw David, his favorite man-friend. Pretty soon we were three adults circled around a very spoiled dog, passing out ear rubs and back pats.

Suddenly a thousand bass drums pounded across the sky.

My hair stood on end as my feet left the blacktop for a moment.

We looked up at dark clouds with long crackling fingers of lightning poking between them. One hot poker hit the power pole at the end of David's driveway, sparking like Fourth of July and frying the transformer. My first thought was, "There goes the electricity and any chance of being able to bake a cake."

David stepped closer and put his arm around my back. "Are you okay, Josie?"

I smiled. He had my back and Ms. Perfect was driving into the sunset, not that I ever thought David would be anything but a loyal, devoted fiancé. He reminded me that he had agreed to pick me up at four-thirty for Mom's party. He asked me to come inside and see if the cake was okay.

"You bought a cake?"

"No, I baked a cake," he laughed.

"Oh, that's even better," I said, hoping the thing looked and tasted halfway decent. A vision of one of my cakes came to mind, sagging on one side where the frosting slid and collected, and tough and chewy on the other side.

David lit a candle. Even in flickering candlelight, the cake was a beauty. A manly beauty, a perfect two-layer rectangle with dark chocolate frosting flawlessly applied. Perfectly legible yellow lettering, "Happy Birthday, Leola" was centered below a rainbow of sprinkles.

"Are you sure you didn't buy this cake?"

"I'm sure. Did you wrap the present?" he asked, his lips slowly curling into a smile. His eyes twinkled.

"What present? Oh, ah that present." I snatched a tiny finger of frosting. "Wow, this is good!"

David laughed, "I picked up the rose bush while you were out. It's wrapped and in the car."

"Sorry, the nursery work has taken it all out of me," I sighed. "But at least I remembered to buy the rose bush from Jason." It would be the perfect gift for my mom, chairwoman of her rose club and backyard horticulture enthusiast.

On that note, I walked home with Solow. It was only four o'clock but looked and felt much later. I barely had time to primp and dress in the pathetic glow of six candles and a flashlight for Mom's party.

Thunder rumbled outside as I poured kibble into Solow's bowl. He ran down the hall and crawled under my bed.

The doorbell rang.

I blew out the candles, and David and I reluctantly left Solow to his under-the-bed shivering. My poor dog had to stay home because Mom had a rule about no animals in her house, and she let me know that Solow was an animal. Weird.

Thankful for the Miata's low profile, we watched other travelers fighting the wind and slanted rain. My white knuckles held the cake encased in a rectangular-shaped plastic dome. The rose bush shared the passenger seat leg space.

Suddenly David braked as the delivery truck we were following swerved to miss a rush of deeper water cutting across the road. It careened to the right, coming to a stop against the hillside. In large letters across the back of the truck, "WildWest Nursery," had not reached my attention until that moment.

"David, pull over!" I shouted.

We came to a full stop about ten yards in front of the truck.

Traffic swished by.

Oily water splattered David's door.

I opened my door, unhooked my pant legs from Ms. Rose, set the cake on the seat and turned to see if Jason was okay. His truck was already rolling forward, as he looked for a chance to reenter the flow of traffic. Feeling thankful that my boss was okay, I settled into the passenger seat. We continued our trip to Santa Cruz.

It was dark when we arrived at Mom and Dad's 1940's restored bungalow on Walnut Street in downtown Santa Cruz. The wild rainstorm had subsided but Ms. Rose was stronger than ever, hanging onto my pant leg as I tried to leave my seat. David circled the car and plucked the cake from my lap, leaving both my hands free to fight off Ms. Rose. I finally gave up, pulled rose out of the car and walked up to the house with her thorny little arms still clinging to my pant leg.

Dad and the next-door neighbor, Myrtle, were in full party-mode as they greeted us and took turns trying to set me free of Ms. Rose. Dad had invited a group of guys wearing shiny blue and gold bowling uniforms with matching party hats. Prompt and dressed to kill, the ladies from Mom's rose club proffered their ideas on how to keep from being tortured by unruly thorns. A little late!

The rest of the mob consisted of a collection of oldsters who, for the most part, were active in sports, recreation, charity clubs and civic duties. They were a noisy bunch that arrived on time and enjoyed pulling off a good surprise party. Sadly, they assumed Mom was turning eighty (who counts every candle) because most people don't have a big seventy-ninth birthday party. Dad thought it would be the ultimate surprise, until Mom came home. Aunt Clara and Uncle Bill were nicely dressed and Mom wore her red sari, pearl earrings and gold sandals.

Which begs the question…what did she know and when did she know it?

Chapter 8

David and I had discussed attending services at the Aromas Community Church Sunday; but when Sunday morning arrived, I remembered David's toothache the night before. It seems he had a chipped molar that needed attention. With Dad's cooperation, poor sweet David had medicated himself with whiskey. Consequently, I drove the two of us home from Mom's party. I could only imagine how he would feel in the morning.

The house was quiet except for Solow's steady breathing as he slept in his doggy bed across the room from me.

It was my chance to sleep a little longer.

Around eight I woke up from a dream where David was lying on his back and I was straddling his chest with pliers in my hands, pulling at his broken molar—desperate to keep the dentist, Ms. Perfect, away. Solow licked David's feet, making him laugh while I worked.

When I was fully awake, I realized Solow was licking my foot.

"Are you telling me you're hungry, or is it that Fluffy's outside waiting for you?" I decided to let Solow out for a Fluffy chase. While he was out, I showered, dressed and pushed Mr. Coffee's buttons. While sipping coffee and feeling thankful to Pacific Gas & Electric for fixing the power outage, I remembered something Myrtle told me at the party. Rather than let it fester, I decided to call around and see if what she said was true.

Alicia picked up on the second ring.

"Good morning, Jo. Isn't it a beautiful day?"

"Yeah, I guess so. Allie, can you check your computer for some information? There's a rumor going around that Jason was thrown out of the rodeo business for cheating."

"And if he could cheat, maybe he could also commit murder?" she said.

"I guess you could say that."

"Why don't you ask Jason?"

"I will, I just want to research it first," I said, not wishing to get tangled up with my old Mac computer any time soon. Alicia was able to find things quickly while I usually had trouble with the basic mechanics of the machine. She knew how computer-challenged I was and agreed to do a search. We hung up.

Solow and I had a hearty breakfast, I cleaned the kitchen, and we walked over to David's house to see how he was feeling. I had never seen him with blood-shot eyes before. Pale and unshaven, he looked more like road kill than the beautiful man I was used to seeing.

"Josie, if I'd known you were coming over I'd have baked a cake," he laughed. But his face didn't look happy as he pressed an ice pack to his cheek.

"Oh my gosh, I know what will take away your pain...." I twirled around and was out the door before David could sputter one word. I charged up the gentle slopes of Otis Road, passing by fourteen mailboxes, two feral cats and one gopher with his head sticking out of a hole. Solow ignored the cats and the gopher as he struggled to keep up with me, long body bouncing, ears flying. He knew we were on a mission.

Approaching Jason's house, Solow sniffed and then marked the left front wheel on Jason's dusty black pickup truck.

Jason burst out the front door carrying a file folder full of papers.

"Hey, Jo," he waved, "I'm on my way back to work."

"Okay, we're just out for a walk," I explained. "Thought I'd check on Lito."

"See ya tomorrow." He backed up his truck as Solow and I rounded the big house and knocked on Lito's door. I didn't wait for the young man to open it. We just walked in.

The sofa was empty.

"Hey, Lito, it's Josephine," I said, peeking into Caitlin's bedroom and then the bathroom. "Solow, where's Lito?" I picked up his *Mechanics Illustrated* magazine and let him sniff it. Next to the magazine was the little roll-on painkiller. I tucked it in my Levi pocket and we went outside. Solow sniffed his way to the back of the little house where an empty horse arena quietly displayed a scattering of mud puddles from recent storms. He sniffed all around the corral, a barn and a tool shed, then turned around and headed back to the front of the house and down the driveway past the neighbor's mailbox with 'Molly Pearson' written in black letters on the side.

Little Richard was in my head as my heart pounded to the beat of, "Good Golly, Miss Molly." We pounded the pavement all the way back to David's house. Gulping air, I quickly told David about Lito not being at home.

"The poor boy is injured...." I stammered.

"Maybe he went somewhere with his mother," David offered.

"The only place Lito would go is to the doctor...on a Sunday?"

"That's a good point, but I'm sure there's a good explanation...."

"David, Caitlin and Lito are hiding from someone. She dyed her hair black. I saw her blond roots."

"Roots don't mean anything," he said, sitting with his long legs stretched the length of the couch.

"Black hair doesn't suit her. I think it's her disguise."

David groaned.

"Oh, I almost forgot. I brought you something for pain." I removed his slippers and applied a couple of drops to the bottom of one foot.

"What is that?"

"Pain medicine. Now hold still while I put some on your other foot."

I put one dot behind each of his ears for good luck.

A couple of minutes later, David's shoulders dropped and the lines across his forehead disappeared. He closed his eyes and fell asleep. I covered his legs with a lap blanket. Even at his worst, David still looked wonderful to me. I bent down and kissed his forehead.

His eyes fluttered.

"Are you asleep?" I said softly.

His lip twitched, then curled into a smile.

"Thanks, Josie, my tooth is much better. I didn't get much sleep last night so I think I'll catch a few winks."

"Okay, see you later," I said, on my way to the front door. David was obviously relaxed and feeling better, but Lito was missing.

The house phone rang as I walked through my back door, Solow at my heels. I grabbed the phone but not in time. It had gone silent. The first three numbers of the caller were 415, but I didn't catch the rest of it. I told Solow it was just as well—probably a robo-selling-something call since they didn't leave a message.

I dialed Alicia. She picked up right away.

"Allie, you always have your head on straight...."

"Jo, just tell me what's going on. You sound like you're a wreck."

"I told you about Lito falling and hurting his tail bone. Well, now he's missing. How can he be missing when he can barely walk?"

"Does his mother know?"

"I don't think so. I wanted to call her at the nursery, but I don't have the number."

"I know, you want me to look it up for you. It's your lucky day, I'm already sitting at my computer and here's the number."

"Thanks, Allie, you're a doll."

I dialed the nursery and started to panic on the fourth ring.

"WildWest Nursery, Caitlin speaking, how can I help you?"

"Caitlin, it's Josephine. Was Lito supposed to go somewhere today?"

"I'm sorry Josephine, I have several customers here…I didn't catch what you said about Lito."

"I asked you if Lito was going anywhere today…."

"Of course not. Hang on…." The old cash register cha-chinged and I heard Caitlin count out the change. "Sorry, Josephine, it's crazy around here. Did you say you're looking for Lito?"

"I've already been up to your place to see how he's doing, but he's not there."

After a long silence, Caitlin said, "I think I know what happened. Thank you for calling." She hung up.

I turned to Solow. "She hung up! Can you believe that? What kind of mother is she?"

Solow looked at the floor as if he were being scolded.

"Sorry, Sweetie, I didn't mean to rant." I grabbed a fast sandwich and tossed Solow a couple bites. "Want a ride in the truck?"

Solow instantly ran to the front door, tail wagging.

I grabbed my purse and we took off for WildWest Nursery. Staying home doing nothing was not an option. My nerves couldn't take it. I needed to know what happened to Lito.

WildWest Nursery should have been called WildWest Circus because the parking lot was full. I parked at the side of the road behind a string of customer vehicles. As Solow and I walked across the parking lot, I watched Jason load prickly cacti into the back of an older Ford Explorer.

Moving along to the gift shop, I found Caitlin ringing up two flats of succulents. Her eyes were red, her jaw set. She looked up.

"Josephine, I'll be done in a minute. Can you please help this lady carry her mini palm tree to the car?" She pointed to a petite senior standing beside her palm tree.

"Yeah, sure," I said, lifting an indigo-glazed ceramic pot containing a four-foot tall chubby palm tree onto a flatbed cart. Lifting the tree from the cart into the back of the woman's SUV was a bigger challenge yet. The little lady thanked me and drove away.

I loosened the tension in my back by bending at the waist and touching my toes a few times.

"Josephine, I need some help!" Jason shouted, holding his wrist.

I straightened up and trotted over to him. The first thing I noticed was blood on his jacket sleeve. Before I reached Jason, I had to quickly step out of the way of the Ford Explorer leaving the parking lot in a hurry.

"What's the matter, Jason? Cactus get your tongue?"

"It wasn't my tongue and it wasn't from a cactus," he grumped. "I need you to get me an ice pack from the gift shop cooler. My thumb's killing me."

"How did that happen?"

"The Jackass slammed his trunk while I had my hand in it. I pulled everything out but my thumb." He showed me a cut running parallel to his paper cut.

"How bout we wash it first...?"

"No time for that, just bring ice."

"Okay, boss," I said over my shoulder. I entered the shop, grabbed the ice pack from the cooler and started to leave.

"Okay, Josephine, I have a moment...." Caitlin said.

"I'll be back," I said, as I walked outside. Jason was already loading a dozen chrysanthemums into a white Jeep. I waited until he was finished.

"Thanks, Josephine." He immediately wrapped the pack around his hand.

"Jason, I think I can help you with that pain."

He glared at me.

"No joke," I said. "I can help you." I pulled the little roll-on wonder from my Levis pocket, popped off the cap and quickly dabbed a drop behind Jason's ear. As I tried to reach the other ear, he swatted my hand.

"What are you doing?" he demanded.

"This stuff really works...."

"In the first place, it's my thumb, not my ear that hurts."

"I know that. Would you like a drop on your wrist?"

"Okay, okay, forget it. Tell me why you're here," he said, as we pushed flatbed carts into their stall.

"I'm here because I need to talk to Caitlin."

Jason tilted his head to one side. "Actually, my thumb is better. That's weird."

I walked away before another emergency happened.

A customer drove out of the lot. Gravel pelted my ankles.

In the distance, Bea tromped across acres of potted baby trees, while a young couple inspected hedge greenery. Entering the shop, I found Caitlin ringing up another customer. An old gentleman with a cane occupied Bea's chair, so I puttered around the shop straightening shelves full of birdhouses and decorative pots until Caitlin was finally free. Solow sat beside the old man, loving the attention.

"It was sweet of you to come all the way to Gilroy to talk to me," Caitlin said. "I'm afraid we can't get Lito back for a while—not until my next court date. His father's been looking for us."

"Oh, that's awful," I said, wishing I could think of something comforting to say to her. "I have an extra coffee pot if you'd like to have it."

"Wow, that would be great. Thank you, Josephine. Are you clocking in today or just visiting?"

"To tell you the truth, I don't have a plan. I guess I could help out for a while." Three more customers inched their way into the little shop, as an older couple left with their baby magnolia tree and a shingled birdhouse.

Caitlin rang up a holly tree for the old man in the chair. She suggested I carry the tree, four feet of mean scratchiness accosting me from every angle, out to his vehicle. The old man walked to his car with the help of a cane while I loaded little Ms. Holly into the trunk, hoping all the dirt wouldn't fall out of the pot as she lay on her side. The man slowly worked his way into the driver's seat, turned the key, backed up, tapped another car lightly, put the car in drive and sprayed gravel everywhere as he melted into traffic heading east.

Bea was making a beeline for her chair as I entered the shop. I moseyed over to her and began a casual conversation.

"What do you mean askin' me bout my brother? That was ten years ago, and the newspapers got it all wrong," Bea snapped. "Jason quit because he was gettin' too old to bust them broncos."

"I heard...."

"Who gives a fiddle what you heard." Bea's fat cheeks had turned red. "Jason's problem was that he had some shifty friends. One so-called friend said my brother put a burr under his saddle. Bad stuff was always happening on the circuit. He's better off here."

Time passed quickly at the WildWest Circus with so many customers and problems to solve. Bea left early and Jason had his hands full with several deliveries, so it was up to Caitlin and me. She had a handle on plant names, and I did most of the cha-chings at the register.

After the last customer left, a little after six o'clock, Jason locked the shop gate and then the parking lot gate. Caitlin and I drove into Gilroy for some Pieology—build-your-own pizza. Now that there was no one to go home to, she was perfectly willing to have dinner with me, while Solow napped in my truck.

"Josephine, thanks for checking on Lito." She stared at her pizza as if it were two-week-old boiled smelt.

"No problem," I said. "He's a good kid. Is Lito going to be all right staying with his father?"

"I think so." Caitlin took a deep breath and looked at the ceiling. "I don't think Lito liked living in Aromas, separated from his friends. He might have called his father."

"How do you like living in Aromas?"

"I kind of like living in the country but I miss my house in Gilroy. It was a good neighborhood—lots of nice people. Not like Jason's mother...."

"What was wrong with his mother?" I asked.

"Just grumpy and old fashioned. She didn't want us to move into the cottage, probably because she already knew the house had been sold to her favorite daughter, Fern. Jason didn't know about the sale yet and insisted we move in."

"So how do you know Jason?"

"My ex does promotion work for the rodeos. Writes for the Mercury and does TV ads. I was with him when he interviewed Jason a few years ago, back in his heyday."

Chapter 9

Nightmares featuring bucking broncos chasing Solow, dressed as clowns, kept me busy half the night. I woke up Monday exhausted and sweaty. Early morning light revealed that Solow was sleeping happily in his bed—no bucking horses anywhere. I decided the best way to shake off the angry horse images was to have a shower and a good breakfast. After all of that, I felt much better. If I had been married to David, things would have been different. He would have calmed me down and shown me how silly my dreams were. But we hadn't set a wedding date yet, so the powerful image of an angry stallion lived on in my fertile imagination.

At work, Solow was proving to be a chick-magnet. WildWest customers, especially the women, loved to pet his velvety ears and watch him bounce along the paths lined with potted plants, shrubs and trees. He followed me around the property and napped on the welcome rug when I worked at the cash register. People just stepped over him.

When Caitlin arrived at nine-thirty, I went to work on the mural.

Solow sunned himself near my feet until Alicia drove into the parking lot. Suddenly he was wide awake and happy to see a friend.

"What do you want me to do, Jo?" Alicia said, climbing out of her green Volvo looking fresh and sparkly as usual. Somehow, her work clothes never had paint on them, while mine had colorful smudges everywhere.

"Allie, I'm so glad you could make it. Here's some chalk and the level. You need to draw a sign up there." I pointed to the upper center part of the long mural wall. "And then paint it black and green like the sign on the van over there." I pointed to the van I had driven to Milpitas on my first day of work. "The sign should be about six feet long and about two feet high."

A row of concrete bump-stops kept WildWest customers from smashing into our ladders. We had a workspace of three feet between the wall and the bumpers. Alicia used the six-foot ladder and I used my little three-footer for painting the long stretch of foothills. California has always been known for its golden hills, especially in summer and fall. I imagined my golden hills with patches of green grass, the two colors representing the changing of seasons. And I pictured fat cows filling their bellies with green grass.

At ten o'clock, Bea's hatchback rolled to a stop, tapping my ladder and shaking my confidence. The back of the car was stuffed full of boxes, again. She lumbered into the gift shop and a few minutes later, Caitlin left the shop to work outside. Customers arrived and left, and finally it was lunchtime.

"Jo, where can we go for lunch around here?" Alicia asked.

"If we drive into Gilroy there's all kinds of...sorry, Allie. I'm gonna skip lunch this time. You go ahead," I said, taking two steps down off the ladder. I scampered over to Bea's vehicle as she started the engine. The passenger door opened and I was in.

"What the blazes are you doin?" Bea yelled at me.

"I didn't get an invitation so I just hopped in. I'll buy you some lunch." I settled into my seat and fastened the seatbelt. "Are we going to your dad's house?"

"I am. You can stay in the car," she crabbed.

"Did you get the brakes fixed?"

"Yeah, and I bought a hundred shares of Apple."

"Can't Jason help you out?"

"I ain't no charity case. You can shut up or git out."

The car rolled into a four-way stop sign situation, its front end clearly into the crosswalk. Bea looked at me, her squinty eyes daring me to say something. After a long silence, she turned right and drove about a mile to a gated tract of houses perched on a knoll overlooking Gilroy's flat urban sprawl. We parked in front of a one-story stucco house that looked a lot like all the other houses, each painted in its own shade of brown ranging from mocha to chocolate smoothie. The mocha house had white trim and a magenta door.

"Get off your duff and help me," Bea ordered, popping open the hatch and pulling out box after box of her mother's personal belongings. One over-stuffed cardboard box full of skeins of yarn and knitted items popped open.

"Did your mother knit all this stuff? Oh, look at this adorable hat, and a scarf to go with it. Turquoise, my favorite color!" I gushed. "It even has a little tag sewn into the cap that says, "An Oeblick Original.""

"If you like it, keep it. Now, help me carry the boxes," Bea nagged.

I set the hat and scarf ensemble next to my purse in the passenger seat, and carried one box up to the front door. I rang the bell.

"What do ya think yer doin'? You idiot!" she hissed. "We just leave the stuff right here. Let them worry about it."

"Sorry, Bea, just trying to help...."

The door opened. A heavy set woman wearing a frizzy blue bathrobe and her wet hair wrapped in a towel stood glaring at Bea. A wheelchair rolled up behind Ms. Wethead, who hadn't said a word. She just turned and walked back down the hall.

"Bea, you've come for a visit?" the white whiskered old man said.

"Dad, this is Josephine…and here's Ma's junk." She placed the box she was carrying on the entry floor. I followed suit, placing my box next to hers. The man sat there watching as we made two more trips, filling the entry with four more boxes.

"You have time for a cup of coffee….?" the old man asked.

"No, Dad, I work for a livin'." Bea turned and walked out with me at her heels.

She fired up the car and burned some rubber backing out of the driveway.

"So that was pleasant," I said, cinching my seat belt.

"You think that's bad, sometimes we really get into it," Bea said, her eyes on the road. "Ever since Jason's old lady ran off with Dad, we don't have much use for him or her."

"Why did the woman go with your dad?"

"Money. Dad was divorced, throwin' money around, bein' stupid. I guess she thought that was cool. Besides, Jason was traveling a lot with rodeo work."

"Poor Jason," I said.

"Yeah," she sighed.

Sad thoughts stayed with me all the way into Gilroy. Nasty and hot-tempered as she was, I felt sorry for Bea. She seemed to carry a defensive wall around her.

We stopped at the Pieology restaurant where we built our own personal size pizzas. We ate them passionately, ignoring drips of sauce and grease, neither of us in a hurry to get back to the nursery. Why is it when something tastes especially good, we eat faster? I tried to slow down and make the meal last longer. It looked like Bea was doing the same thing. At least we had one thing in common—love of pizza.

"So, Bea, what about your mom?"

"What about her? She's dead, or didn't you get the memo?"

"I just thought you might like to talk about her…."

"Pizza's gone. Let's go," she snapped.

Road noise was a welcome passenger as we rode back to the nursery. Attempting to park her car, Bea aimed the bumper-less hatchback at my ladder. Thanks to the concrete berm, she barely tapped the ladder.

Alicia's jaw dropped as she watched from her perch.

Caitlin shot out of the gift shop looking around to see what crashed.

Bea put the car in reverse and pulled the car back a few inches so that I'd be able to move my ladder around. I was surprised at the thought and cooperation she had demonstrated—for once.

Jason's delivery truck pulled to a stop along side Bea's car. While she and Jason chatted, I followed Caitlin into the shop.

"Any word from Lito?" I asked.

Her red-rimmed eyes glistened. "No, but I'm sure he'll call me tonight. Did I tell you he's scheduled to have surgery on his left ear next week? I only hope he's home by then."

"What's the surgery for?" I asked.

"Lito has scar tissue in his ear after the last operation. He's back to being completely deaf in his left ear." She looked at the floor. "It took two months to get this new appointment. At least he has a good right ear."

"That's too bad," I said. "I'll work in the shop if you want to take a lunch break."

Caitlin thanked me and walked quickly to her truck.

Jason rounded the corner and entered the shop.

"Jason, Caitlin left her purse. Do you mind if I leave for a few minutes?"

"You're on mural time—go ahead."

I grabbed the red leather bag, dashed over to my truck and fired up the engine. Caitlin had already merged into traffic heading east to Gilroy. I was three cars behind her and anxious to catch up to her. Would she go to lunch or would she go looking for Lito? Up ahead I saw her red pickup turn right. I followed her past Bea's father's mocha house and up two more blocks to a chocolate smoothie two-story stucco with a black door and trim.

Caitlin parked in the driveway. I parked at the curb. She walked up to the front door. I came up behind her with the purse. She turned her head and realized for the first time that she had left her bag behind. She started to thank me when the front door swung open a few inches, and Lito peeked out.

"Hey, Mom, Jo, guess what?" He pushed the door wide open. "I can hear real good with both ears."

"What are you talking about?" Caitlin shook her head, mystified.

"It's true. Ever since the bees stung me, I can hear real good. I even tried it with ear phones," he grinned. "You can cancel my operation."

"That's wonderful, sweetheart, now get your things and I'll drive you home."

"You don't believe me, do you?" he said, pulling his cell phone from his pants pocket. "I Googled it. Bee venom can actually dissolve scar tissue."

"Okay, okay, I believe you. Now, let's go."

Lito stepped back, making room for his dad.

"You don't believe your own kid?" The tall, dark and fairly handsome man said. "And who's this pretty lady?"

"Her name is Josephine. Josephine, this is Chico, my ex."

Chico smiled, exposing a full set of pearly white teeth. "You can have your son in February when he turns eighteen."

The door slammed shut.

Caitlin kicked it.

I put an arm around her and walked her back to her truck.

"I'm sorry, Caitlin…."

"Thanks, Josephine. I'll be okay," she sniffed. "Let's go grab some lunch."

*****

Back at the nursery, business was picking up. Sunny days were like that. Throw in some cold rain and most people stay home. Caitlin picked up a rake and threw herself into some hard raking.

Alicia had just finished drawing the WildWest sign and was mixing various shades of green paint, trying to match the color used on the logos for the company vehicles.

I mixed three shades of grassy-gold-color paint for the foothills and shaded them with touches of purple. At the end of the day, a stand of eucalyptus reached for the sky at the upper left end of the horizon. On the right stood a far-away barn. Twenty-five feet of hills, a barn and eucalyptus was enough for one day. Besides, it was almost five and getting dark. Time to stow ladders and paint into the warehouse.

Alicia finished applying green paint to the lettering. All she had to do was outline the words with black paint the next day. We left the nursery and caravanned over Hecker Pass. She drove into Watsonville and I turned left, heading to Aromas. Stars twinkled in the black sky as Solow slept beside me, his paws twitching at a furious rate. My truck practically drove itself along the familiar route as I thought about the day's events.

Suddenly I was grinding up my gravel driveway, smelling wood smoke from the chimney and smiling at the thought of David making my little house comfortable. I helped Solow down from his seat, and we trotted up the stairs and across the porch. The front door opened and Solow let out a howl directed at his favorite man-friend. I didn't howl, but I let my sweetie know I was happy to see him.

"Hi, Josie, how was work?" He smiled, melting my heart completely with a warm hug.

"It was kinda fun. I painted hills, trees and a barn and helped out with nursery work here and there. The day flew by, and we had the best pizza...."

"Oh, before I forget, a woman named Fern was here looking for you about a half an hour ago."

"I wonder what she wants." I scratched my head. "Fern is Jason and Bea's sister." I remembered the well-dressed tall, skinny redhead...the exact opposite of Bea.

"Fern said she had just come from Jason's house looking for Bea," he added.

"If I had Fern's number I would tell her to look in the tool shed."

"Huh?"

"Well, that's where we found Bea the last time she was missing."

We snuggled up on the couch like two oysters in a shell, Solow at our feet. "This fire makes the house so cozy. Is that wonderful baking smell coming from the kitchen?"

"Yep, are you hungry?"

"Of course I am," I laughed.

"Oh, I just remembered something," he said, pulling a business card out of his shirt pocket. "Fern left this for you."

"You're sure she didn't leave it for you?" I giggled.

David's dark eyes twinkled as he handed over the card.

I dialed Fern's number.

"Hello, Josephine?"

"Yeah, hi, Fern, I hear you're looking for Bea."

"Actually, I want to know where all my mom's stuff went."

"Bea and I delivered it to your dad today. Is anything wrong?"

"Great, now I have to deal with the old man," she growled, and hung up.

Chapter 10

Lying in bed Tuesday morning, all warm and cozy, I thought about oak trees, grazing cows and where I would paint the shadows. I decided it would be morning with the sun coming from the east, casting shadows under and to the left of each cow and tree. I pictured everything in my mind including David riding a bucking horse. And then I thought about him without the horse.

Solow was not in a lounging mood. He sat near my bed watching me with sad blood-shot eyes. When his stare became too much, I climbed out of bed and let him out the back door for a Fluffy chase. Through the kitchen window, I watched him bounce over acres of new green winter grass, ears flapping like a gooney bird trying to fly.

David's prissy white cat, Fluffy, stayed just a few leaps ahead of Solow. When she tired of the chase, she leaped onto a fence post and watched him lumber back home in disgrace for the millionth time.

As soon as breakfast was over, Solow and I climbed aboard the old Mazda pickup and put Aromas twenty-five miles behind us. In front of us was a warm September-like sun. It looked like we were in for a patch of summer weather, which suited me just fine since I had an outdoor mural to finish. I parked the truck between Alicia's Volvo and Bea's bumper-less abomination, and followed Solow as he trotted toward the gift shop and the sound of females arguing.

"Slap!"

"You slapped me!"

"Yeah, Fern, and I'll do it again if ya don't back off."

"You're scaring the dog!"

"The only scaredy cat is you, Fern. What's your problem?" Bea pushed her less than lovely face into a pout, and made a unladylike gesture.

"I don't have a problem, Bea. I just wanted to see Mom's stuff before you gave it all away, okay?" Fern grabbed a garden claw and waved it at her sister. "You need to get that stuff back from Dad, and you should have let me go through it in the first place."

"Yeah, you would look great wearing one of Mom's black knitted shawls," Bea snorted.

Luckily we had yet to see our first customer of the day. I puttered around the place acting like nothing was going on, and found Alicia in the warehouse sorting various sizes of spigots and placing them into their proper bins.

"Good morning, Jo. Are you ready to paint?"

"Sure. Where's Jason?"

"He opened the gates, loaded his truck and took off. And then his sisters arrived." Alicia rolled her eyes and we both laughed.

We hauled our equipment outside. Alicia climbed her ladder. I worked with both feet on the ground, painting golden pastureland and meadows of green grass where oak trees congregated. As I worked, I listened to the sisters trying to work out their differences. Finally, Fern slammed the door of her late-model black Mercedes, jammed it into reverse and stomped on the gas sending gravel flying our way.

Alicia put her hands in front of her face while balancing on the ladder. I crouched down, hands over my head as little rocks pelted the mural wall. We survived the attack without injury but still had an irate woman to deal with. Bea was still fuming an hour later when I walked through the shop on my way to the restroom.

"You got any sisters?" Bea asked, as I tried to hurry past her.

"No, I'm an only child," I said.

She stepped in front of me. "My stupid sister wants all of Mom's knitting junk. Says she's taking up knitting. And my name isn't 'Stupid.' She's up to somethin'," Bea barked.

"So what are you going to do?" I asked, trying to inch my way toward the restroom.

"I'm gonna drive us over to Dad's and pick up the box with all them knitting things in it, just to get Fern off my back. And I'll spring for lunch."

I looked at Bea for a moment trying to figure out who was the other half of "us."

"You like tacos?" she asked.

"Ah, sure, but Alicia and I had planned to...."

"Don't worry 'bout a thing—I'm buyin'," Bea smiled. "I need you to go with me cause the old man's woman won't open the door for me, and if I don't get that knittin' junk, Fern'll never leave me alone."

Quickly mulling over my options, I decided to go with Bea since she had already given me a beautiful hat and scarf set. And I wanted to check out her dad and his woman concerning the murder issue. And why irritate the 'Bea' if I didn't have to?

Alicia, always the mature level-headed person in any group, sounded like she understood my predicament. Even though she was fifteen years younger than I, she always seemed to be thirty years wiser.

Jason pulled his delivery truck to a stop in the parking lot.

Caitlin worked in the gift shop where an old couple was paying for several sacks of fertilizer.

Jason hefted the sacks into an old farm truck and told Bea to take her lunch break.

I offered to drive, but Bea said she would not impose on me and insisted on paying for everything—tacos and gasoline. This news did not make me happy, but I climbed into her car anyway. Bea must have been hungry, because she put eating before seeing her dad. We rolled up to the ordering spot at Jack-in-the-Box. She ordered their special—four tacos for a total cost of two dollars—a no frills package that included no fries or drinks. She over-shot the pick-up window, put the car into reverse and backed into the bumper of the SUV following us.

"Don't follow so close!" she hollered at the driver behind us.

She quickly paid the two dollars, grabbed the bag of tacos and sped away, one hand on the wheel and a taco in the other.

I hung onto the passenger door with white knuckles and ate with my left hand as taco juices ran down to my elbow, and my tummy did back-flips. By the time we reached the mocha house with the red door, our tacos were gone. As we rolled down the driveway, Bea wiped grease off her chin with a napkin. The right front tire flattened a rose bush just before the car came to a complete stop against the corner of the house.

After two tacos and some whiplash, I was happy to see the front door open. I needed to use a restroom.

"Guess we won't be knockin'," Bea snarked, as she climbed out of the car.

I was already taking the front steps two at a time.

"Oh, it's you. I should have known," the woman of the house snapped. She wore grey sweats and had her dark hair pulled back in a ponytail. Her large features were situated on a small narrow face atop a well-fed body.

"So what's it to ya?" Bea said, charging past the woman and into the house. "Hey, Dad, where are you?"

"Who's there, Daphne?"

"Your, daughter, the stupid one," Daphne yelled.

The old man turned a corner in his wheelchair.

"Bea, you're back."

"Yeah, don't get used to it. Josephine's here too." Bea pointed down the hall to the guest bath. "Fern's got her undies in a twist. She thinks she wants Mom's knittin' stuff. Where'd ya put it?"

Daphne smiled and then covered her smile with one large hand.

"Daph, where's the box?" the old man asked.

"I took everything to the Good Thrift Store yesterday, just like you wanted."

"Oh, yeah," he said, stroking his silky white beard. "That's too bad, Bea, we thought you didn't want that stuff."

"I don't want nothin,' but Fern does. She went ballistic on me this mornin.' I'm just tryin' to get her outta my hair."

I listened to the conversation from inside the bathroom, taking my time about coming out. It was a family thing and I wasn't family—thank God! When I finally came out of hiding Bea stood at the front door, anxious to leave. Her dad seemed a little sad to see her go. We climbed into her car, and I braced myself for another wild ride, this time to the Good Thrift Store.

"Whatcha think of Daaaph-nee?" Bea asked me, mimicking the voice of a cranky teenager.

"I like her name...."

"Are you kiddin' me?" she said, steering the car around to the back of the Good Thrift Store building. She slipped the old hatchback into a parking space between two soccer mom SUVs, and stomped on the brakes. The car came to a hard stop against a parking berm, sending my head into a quick forward jerk. Directly in front of us, two young men were hauling sacks and boxes of donated items through the back door. Bea asked one of them if we could look through a box that was mistakenly dropped off.

"Lady, you need to go through the front door and ask someone working in the store."

We marched around the building to the front door and entered. The place was huge, full of stuff and close to empty of people. We finally found a frowzy blond hanging shirts on a rack near the back of the store. Bea approached her.

"Hi, I need to take back a box of stuff my father accidentally donated."

Ms. Frowzy stopped her work and glared at Bea.

"But you can keep the other boxes he dropped off," I said.

"I'm so sorry, but our policy is…"

"Lady, I just want my junk!" Bea snapped.

I leaned closer to the woman. "Better give it to her; she's off her meds," I whispered.

Frowzy backed away from us. "The best I can do is let you buy it back."

"What if I ain't got no money?" Bea asked, hands on hips.

"I have a credit card," I said.

"In that case, go through that door and ask Bert to help you."

We quickly walked down the next aisle and through an open door into the back room where two guys were depositing donations to be sorted. Bea spotted her handy-work, six cardboard boxes she had filled with her mom's stuff.

"Can one ah you guys help me here?" she yelled at the men.

A third fellow came out of the adjacent lunchroom. He strolled over to Bea, said his name was Bert, and asked what he could do for her. By that time, she had opened three of the six boxes.

"Ma'am, how can I help you?"

"My mom's stuff was accidentally donated and I want some of it back...."

"I'm afraid our policy doesn't cover that...."

"I WANT MY MOM'S STUFF. Are you hard of hearing?" she asked.

I sidled up to the guy. "Be careful, she's off her meds."

He looked angry as he started to walk away.

"Hey," I said, "we'll pay for what we take back."

He whipped around with dollar signs in his pale blue eyes. From there it was easy, all we had to do was pay an exorbitant amount of money and load the designated box into the car. Supporting myself had never been an easy job, especially with people like Bea around.

We cruised through Gilroy, a town of 55,000 people, and hopped onto Highway 101 heading north toward Morgan Hill with a population of 45,000.

"Bea, why are we going in this direction?"

"I just want to drop this junk off at Fern's...."

"But I'm supposed to be painting...."

"Don't get yer dee-signer painty pants on fire, it won't take long. She lives in Morgan Hill."

I was happy to hear that Fern lived in the closest town to Gilroy, just ten minutes away, unless the freeway was stopped up. And it was. The ten-minute commute turned into forty-five minutes of wasted time. But it could have been worse. With Bea's bad brakes we could easily have been like the three-car wreck we passed that had held us up. It was slow and go, getting to the third Morgan Hill exit, with Bea driving in low gear in the slow lane and pumping the brakes constant-ly.

The third Morgan Hill exit was Cochran. It took us through the northwest end of town and up into the hills where every house was the size of a castle and had a view of the valley below. Bea putted up Hill Street and parked at the curb in front of a very large two-story modern Victorian with a four-car garage. At first glance, I knew it was a house but not a home, too perfect to be lived in.

Bea climbed out of her car and opened the hatch in the back. She came back to the curb carrying a red brick, bent down and placed it behind the back right tire.

"What are you doing?" I asked.

"Don't you know nothin'? We're on a slope here."

Bea was right. The little car could have rolled for miles if it was allowed to.

She nodded toward the box of knitting. "Carry the box up to the front door...I need a drink of water." Bea went to the side of the house, pulled a length of hose from it's housing, turned on the water and drank. She came back to the car with a large wet spot on the front of her shirt.

I left the box on the porch, pushed up against the front door.

Bea loaded her brick into the car, and we took off for Gilroy using the back roads—a very scenic forty-five minute drive. But who was counting?

"Bea, what exactly does Fern do for a living?"

"She's a nuclear physicist...."

"Very funny," I snorted.

"She is, but she works at Chipcoe, a chip company."

"That's really funny. A scientist making potato chips, or are they corn chips?"

"Not potato or corn chips, you idiot. They make them tiny, tiny chips for cars, trains, planes and boats. Pretty soon we won't need no people to drive stuff any more, just microchips."

My eyes looked up at the ceiling as I whispered to myself, "Praise God, no more drivers like Bea."

Bea's car thunked to a stop against a berm at WildWest Nursery. Alicia's frightened look evaporated as we climbed out of the car and stood next to her ladder admiring the sign. A couple more strokes and she would be finished.

"Is it okay if I pay you when Jason pays me?" I asked.

Alicia smiled, "Don't worry, I can wait."

I knew she would be fine with a later payment. Her professor-husband supported the family very well. Alicia's earnings were for extras, like entertainment, trips and such. As a young child, she sold chewing gum in the streets of Tijuana to stay alive. At age seven, Alicia was adopted by an American couple and later married into a good family.

From those thoughts, my mind moved on to the Oeblick murder and an old saying, "Follow the money."

If I followed the Oeblick family's money, where would it lead?

The old man lived in a nice house and Daphne looked happy to be spending his money. Jason didn't seem to have a house of his own, and not even one horse. Fern obviously had plenty of money and a great job while Bea seemed to have almost nothing. Did that mean that Bea or Jason murdered their mother over money? I couldn't even imagine it.

My stomach growled. Two little tacos would not get me through the afternoon. I watched Alicia drive away, noticing that the sun was already low in the sky. Maybe I should just go home and start fresh the next day.

Chapter 11

Middle of the week, hump-day Wednesday, started out bright and sunny like Solow's disposition. Always ready to travel, he howled goodbye to Aromas and barked hello WildWest Nursery.

Bea and Jason were handling the nursery work, as Caitlin had taken the day off.

Just two hours into my work, painting meadows and oaks, Solow thumped his tail and howled.

A familiar voice told me I missed a spot. I turned around.

"Lito, what are you doing here?"

"My dad usually works out of his office at home, but he had to go to a meeting in San Francisco," Lito smiled, "so I hitched a ride over here."

"What about your tailbone?"

"I'm better, as long as I don't have to sit." He reached down to pet Solow. "Don't worry, I'll be fine. I just wanted to see how you paint your murals. I was a pretty good art student in high school and painting is what I love to do."

"Are you saying you'd like to paint for a living?" I asked.

"Yep. Anything you want me to paint for you?"

"Yeah, see that group of eucalyptus trees on the left?" I pointed to the little trees I had already painted. "I'd like another three or four trees beside the barn. They'll be slightly bigger, making them look closer." I reached over and placed my hand where the trees would go.

"I'm on it," Lito said, as he set himself up with paint and brushes. A couple hours later, there were three eucalyptus trees on one side of the barn and a tractor on the other. Lito had accomplished realism without being too tight.

"A few highlights on that tractor would be nice."

"I'm on it," he said. "I'm thinking about taking some art classes at Gavilan College. What do you think?"

"I think that's an excellent idea, Lito. Besides cultivating your artistic talent, you'll need determination— through thick and thin. Half the population thinks they're artists, but only the ones who persevere succeed. You seem like a guy who can make it in the art world."

"Thanks for the encouraging words, Josephine. Wish my dad...."

"My folks wanted me to be a secretary. Can you see me doing that?" I asked Lito. "Dress up everyday, sit at a desk and mind my P's and Q's?"

He laughed, "No way."

"You have to follow your heart, Lito. Actually you're lucky, you know what you want to do at a young age. Maybe you can go with your dad's plan and take art classes on the side. Eventually, he'll see how talented you are."

"I doubt that," he said, painting a shadow under a tractor approximately the size of a cell phone.

"Are you in contact with your mom?"

"Sure, I call her everyday. A few more months and I'll be living with her again, or get a place of my own."

"I hate to tell you this, but your mural business needs time to build...."

"Just kidding about 'my own place.' I know how much rents are around here. But maybe I can help Mom out with the rent." He asked if there was anything else I wanted him to paint. I told him to take a break and call his mom.

The next time I saw Lito, Jason had put him to work at the cash register, and Solow had gone to sleep at his feet.

By one o'clock, I was starving. Gravel crunched behind me. Imagining a taco truck pulling into the parking lot, I dropped my brush in water and turned around ready for a good lunch. Dang! It was that fancy Mercedes of Fern's.

She leaped out of the car, leaving the door wide open and charged over to the gift shop where Bea was minding the register because Lito had hitched a ride with a salesman back to his dad's house.

Three customers scurried out to their cars as Fern and Bea faced off. When I came around the corner, I saw Bea holding a rake in the air, fending off Fern and her hedge clippers. Their shouting traveled all the way out to Jason who was mending the fence between WildWest Nursery and the winery next door. He dropped everything and came running.

Solow ran outside and crawled under my truck.

"She started it," Bea whined.

"All I wanted was the box of knitted stuff from my mom," Fern growled.

"Jason, get her out of here," Bea demanded.

"I'm family. I have a right to be here," Fern screamed.

Jason grabbed the weaponry and asked his sisters to speak to each other calmly, explaining that yelling was not good for business.

Bea calmly explained to Jason that she had delivered the box of knitting supplies to her sister's front door. Fern argued that the box was not there. Bea asked me if the box was there. I nodded that it was. Fern asked why we didn't leave it at the back door since anyone could see the front door from the street and take the box.

"It ain't her jewelry, it's a stupid box of yarn!" Bea said.

"You let someone steal it," Fern said.

That was when the hair pulling started. Jason tried to pull them apart, but they were too angry to be stopped. The taco truck came and went while the ladies wrestled and cursed. I ran after the truck, but the driver didn't see me. I couldn't blame him for wanting out of there in a hurry.

I came back to the shop panting. "What happened?" I asked, looking down at Fern lying on the concrete floor like a lanky rag doll. A trickle of blood made it's way down her forehead, as Jason pulled Fern into a sitting position, swiveled her around and leaned her shoulders against the wall with her sharp chin resting on her chest.

"She hit her stupid head on the birdhouse," Bea said, pointing to an owl box swinging from the ceiling. "Any of them other birdhouses wouldn't have hurt," she chuckled.

Fern opened her yellow-green eyes and slowly lifted her head, groaning. She put a hand up to the trickle of blood, looked at its color and sighed. About ten minutes later, she was awake again and ready to stand up with Jason's help. He warned his sisters not to make any more trouble.

Solow and I piled into my truck. I fired up the engine and took off to go look for lunch. I found the taco truck a block away in the Sarah's Vineyard parking lot. What luck! It was backing up to turn around and leave, so I positioned my pickup behind it and gave them a friendly honk-honk to let them know I was there.

Bumpers tapped, but not hard.

I ordered Jason and Bea's favorite burritos, a taco for Solow and a tostada for myself. I would have ordered something for Fern, but she looked like one of those picky eaters who don't eat much of anything. Besides, she had a great job at Chipcoe, so why waste money on her?

Getting back to the nursery, I was happy to see the Mercedes gone. I hoped Ms. Twiggy was well enough to drive safely.

Jason greeted the burritos and me with whole-hearted pleasure.

"No sodas?" Bea crabbed.

"There's plenty in the cooler," Jason reminded her.

Jason waited on a couple of customers while Bea and I ate our lunches. He carried a sack of potting soil to a woman's car, showed a gentleman where the fruit trees were located, hurried back to the shop and tore into his burrito. His eyes fell on Bea's empty chair.

"Bea said she had business in town and left," I said. "Jason, did anyone come to the house the day your mother was killed, besides Caitlin and Lito?"

"I came home to check on Mom around noon. We had lunch together and then I went back to work—a delivery to Bakersfield," he mumbled, his mouth full of burrito.

"Didn't you tell me you had to go to Santa Barbara that day…?"

"Anyway, Mom was sick and I needed to check on her."

"You were a good son…."

"If I were a good son I would have kept her safe," Jason countered.

"Did you know she was in danger?"

"Not really, but I should have seen the signs."

"Like what?"

"Sometimes I'd hear her speaking Farsi on the phone. As far as I know, she didn't know anyone who spoke Farsi. I can't speak it, but I know it when I hear it because Mom used it when she was mad at Dad. He didn't know what she was saying, so the arguments ended pretty fast." Jason laughed, and took another bite of burrito.

"Did they argue a lot?"

"Not so much, but then my dad quit coming home," Jason said.

"Did your parents get a divorce?"

"Yep, in the settlement Dad got the nursery and Mom got the house."

"So where will you live when the dust settles?"

Jason frowned.

"I'm sorry, Jason, I'm asking too many questions, aren't I?"

"Don't worry about it, Josephine. I own the nursery now and I'll be going back to my house in Gilroy, the one Dad's living in. We'll just switch places."

"But I thought Fern...."

"They went together on it. My dad knew Mom was dying and would never sell the place to him. So Fern buys the house, and when the deals all done, Dad buys it from Fern. The good news is I'll get my house back. A big empty house." Jason stared at a water stain on the concrete floor. "I better go."

Jason pushed a couple of empty carts back to the corral and greeted customers along the way. My next question to him would have been, "Would Jason's wife live with the father in Aromas?" It made me sad to think about Jason's dysfunctional family.

I waited on customers in the gift shop until Bea came back to work two hours later looking like she'd gone for a spin in a clothes dryer. She ran fingers through her tangled grey hair as if that would help her appearance, didn't explain her absence and immediately took a smoke break.

I walked outside into the afternoon sunshine, stood back, took a critical look at the mural and decided it needed another oak tree. I painted the new tree lower, larger and more detailed than the others, making it appear to be closer. Already, the picture had a feeling of depth.

My old pansy customer had parked her car close to where I stood painting.

In my mind, I thanked whoever invented the berm, once again.

Half an hour later, Ms. Pansy proudly carried a two-foot tall potted prickly pear cactus to her car. Instead of getting in, she "yoo-hooed" me to come see her purchase. When I heard her say, "Hello" for the second time I swung around and my shoulder met up with the prickly cactus plant.

"Oh dear, did it bite you?" she whimpered.

"It'll be okay, don't worry," I said, as tears stung my eyeballs. I blinked them away and pretended to myself that I had just received an inoculation against friendly pansy people. I would never let myself cry over a shot.

"I'm so sorry. Now everyone is crying," she said.

"Who else is crying?" I asked, looking around the parking lot.

"The lady who sold me this cactus." She pointed to the gift shop. "I'll be going now."

And not a minute too soon, I thought to myself as I walked over to the shop and peeked inside. Bea sat in her favorite chair guzzling soda pop. A cigarette smoldered on the little glass table next to her. I studied her face, looking for tears, but a clump of grey hair blocked my view. She turned her head a bit and saw me.

"Is everything okay, Bea?"

"Just hunky dory, if it's any ah yer business." Her red-rimmed eyes and blotchy skin looked pretty close to normal, but I did see her lower lip quiver for a second.

Picking up a feather duster, I began dusting the shelves full of glassware, ceramics and carved wood items.

Bea sneezed.

I put the duster down, picked up a potted plant bearing shiny green leaves and little pink ballerina flowers, and immediately set it back down. My left arm was killing me. Jaws clenched, I hurried into the restroom, pulled off my jacket and rolled up my left shirtsleeve to look at my shoulder. I expected to see a crater, but all I saw was a small red mark with a black pinpoint in the middle. How could something that small hurt so much?

Bea leaned her head in the door. "What are you doin?" she exclaimed.

"I was poked by a cactus...."

"You too? You don't see me cryin,'" Bea said. "I just slapped some aloe vera on mine."

"Have any more aloe for me?"

She didn't say a word, just left me standing there. A minute later, Bea was back with a freshly cut slab of gooey aloe vera and five feet of stretchy ankle wrap. She held the slimy side of the plant to my skin, wrapped my shoulder-arm-pit area and secured it with a pin. When I pulled my shirtsleeve over it, I looked like a lop-sided linebacker.

"Bea, it feels better already. Where did you learn to do this?"

"The desert, up there by Vegas."

"How long did you live there?"

"Too long. My old man was a drunkin' gambler and I was a fool. He kicked ma dog and I almost shot him. Too bad I missed."

Chapter 12

Thursday morning started off dark and chilly. Outside my bedroom window, bamboo chimes clattered and crystal chimes tinkled. After Wednesday night's news report, it didn't surprise me to see foul weather moving in on our coastal paradise. What bothered me most was the prospect of rain—enemy number one of outdoor mural painting. In my mind, I had drawn and painted the cowboy and bucking horse at least a dozen times. If worst came to worst, I could always paint the horse and rider a few weeks later, after I finished painting the Gilroy Library mural. But I had a thing about leaving a project before it was finished.

If Thursday's paint-door closed due to rain, maybe the murder mystery-door would open. I would have more time to follow the skimpy leads I had so far, such as Jason's ex-wife living with Jason's father—what other despicable things might Daphne do? Fern had an out-of-control temper when it came to yarn? Bea lived a strange life somewhere—I wasn't sure where or how. Caitlin was secretive, but why? Lito was young, strong and minus an alibi. Jason seemed like a nice guy, but his information didn't add up.

Solow took his morning nap as I prepared myself for a day of painting, or nursery work, or investigating Mrs. Oeblick's murder. In my fifty-year-old opinion of myself, I had good health, an appetite for adventure and the ability to be last-minute flexible. At the last minute, I tossed gloves and rubber boots into the truck.

Heading up Hecker Pass Road while rain drummed the windshield, Solow slept and I worried about weather-related accidents. We arrived at the summit and continued down the dry Santa Clara County eastern side of the mountain. No rain, just flurries of dry leaves in the air. WildWest Nursery had the same conditions—cold, windy and dry.

Parking next to Caitlin's red truck, I cracked a window open an inch and let Solow continue his nap. As I walked the short distance to the gift shop, I realized my flimsy rain jacket would not keep me warm. Strong gusts of icy wind attacked my ears and neck. I shivered, turned back to the truck and pulled my knitted turquoise hat and scarf out from behind the driver's seat, silently thanking Bea for the gift.

Back to the shop I went. Caitlin greeted me and complimented me on my hat and scarf, asking if I had knitted them myself.

"No, if it doesn't involve a paint brush, I probably don't know how to do it," I said. "My whole life has been focused on painting—maybe I need more diversity."

"No, Josephine, we all appreciate your artwork. By the way, would you be able to run into Gilroy? Bea just called to ask Jason for a lift. He's not here yet...."

"I can do that," I said, feeling like the last thing I wanted to do was stand in the wind and paint. "Where is she in Gilroy?"

"I'll ask Jason," she said, already punching in his number.

I stepped out of the shop to see if Solow was okay.

"He says she's in Holiday Park off of Tiller," and then he said, "Good luck."

"Good luck, what's that about?" I asked.

Caitlin shrugged and went back to sweeping the floor where a sack of potting soil had leaked.

Solow seemed happy to be on the road again, if awake and alert meant anything. I took the first exit into Gilroy and stopped at the first cheap gas station. After filling the tank, I walked up to the Quick Mart and asked the proprietor where Holiday Park was located.

He pointed, "Go east on Hecker, turn left on Santa Teresa and then right on Tiller. You can't miss it."

No sooner had I turned onto Tiller, than dark clouds opened up, dumping cold, sideways rain onto Gilroy. The two-lane road passed by neighborhoods far off to our right, open spaces on our left and straight through two feet of water at Silvia's Crossing, overflow from the Uvas Creek. I barely saw the fifty-one acres of Holiday Park because my wipers couldn't keep up with the deluge. As we cruised by an open meadow next to a blurred stand of redwood trees, I happened to see a bumper-less hatchback sitting in a meadow about twenty feet from the road, up to it's hubcaps in mud.

"Hang on, Solow, we have to go back," I said, doing a u-ey in the middle of the road.

Solow howled when he saw someone move inside the little car.

I parked at the side of the road with all four tires still on pavement, the bike lane actually. Hard rain blew in from the West, smacking me square in the face. In one minute, I was drenched. Hunched over, I plodded through sucky mud about twenty feet and tapped on Bea's window.

Her puffy red eyes met mine as she opened her window an inch.

"Hey, need a ride?" I shouted over the roar of the wind.

"Yeah, yeah, what's the big deal? Where's Jason?" Bea snapped, as she climbed out of her car and together we slogged our way over to my truck. She took the seat

Solow had kept warm, and he curled up on the floor with Bea's muddy rubber boots resting on his back.

"How did you get stuck way out here?" I asked.

"It ain't 'way out' for some people, it's just a camp."

"There's a campground here?" I squinted through the watery windshield, searching for any sign of a campground.

"If it's any ah yer business, I know people campin' down by the river, gettin' their stuff washed away right now." She stared at the glove box in front of her, shivering.

"Must be someone close to you to come out here in this weather."

"There ya go, pokin' into stuff again." She pulled her boots off and set them beside Solow. Her mismatched stocking feet rested on his back. "We goin' to the nursery or not?"

"Sure, unless you have errands to run, like finding a tow truck."

"I'll wait for the ground tah dry out, and then I'll drive it right out ah there."

By the time we reached the nursery, the rain had subsided into a light sprinkle, but the air was still icey cold and blowy. There was no way I was going to stand in the wind and try to draw a bucking horse. Even on a nice day it would take some good concentration to get the proportions right.

Jason pulled into the parking lot as Bea and I entered the gift shop.

Solow greeted Jason with a wag of his tail and was rewarded with an ear rub and a doggie biscuit.

"Nice hat," Jason grinned.

"Thanks, I have a scarf that goes with it." I watched Bea making a beeline for the bathroom. "Jason, who lives at the park?" I whispered.

"My niece, Sugarbell, Bea's twenty-year-old daughter." He started to leave, but turned back. "I'll be driving some trees down to Monterey as soon as I get them loaded."

"What would you like me to do, since I'm not painting today?"

"Caitlin's working in the warehouse. If something needs doing, I'm sure you'll know what to do, Josephine. And here comes a customer." He smiled at an elderly woman carrying a rose bush up to the register and walked briskly away. By the time I finished ringing up the rose lady, and Ms. Pansy's birdhouse, and a sack of manure for a gentleman customer, Jason's truck was loaded and leaving the premises.

If only I'd had more time to talk to Jason. Why did Sugarbell live in the park? Or was Jason being a smart aleck?

More customers arrived, and I rang up their purchases. As soon as the shop emptied out, Bea appeared, ready to go to work but not until she had a smoke break. After that, she fell asleep in her chair. All the customers in China couldn't wake her. Once again the place cleared out, and Bea opened her eyes.

"Josephine, why don't you go get us some lunch? I'll watch the shop."

"Okay, I'm getting hungry too. Can I ask you a question?"

"No, but I'm sure you're gonna anyway," Bea crabbed.

"Why did you give me the hat and scarf when you have friends at the park who might need them?"

"Cause my daughter has a million of them things from her grandma. She shares 'em with her friends. All the knitted stuff in the world ain't gonna keep them girls warm and dry."

A customer walked into the shop.

I walked out to the parking lot, fired up my truck, ignoring fresh clods of mud under the dash.

Solow manned the passenger seat window, making sure we didn't miss any food establishments along the way.

I queued up behind several cars moving at a snail's pace toward the take-out window at the local hot dog place. Our turn finally came. I paid the big bucks and sped back to WildWest Nursery with a sack of chili dogs, mustard dogs, one plain dog and French fries. Solow gobbled his plain hot dog while I carried the bag into the shop.

The "ball park" aroma interrupted Bea's nap. Her eyes fluttered.

"That there smells good. Hope it's not dogs...."

"What's wrong with hot dogs?" I asked.

"Nothin'," she grinned.

So Bea had a sense of humor after all—not a big one, but enough to lighten things a bit. She dove into the bag, pulling out one of everything.

Caitlin walked into the shop, removed her gloves, pulled out a nice hot mustard dog and automatically made a monetary donation to the hot dog fund.

When it was my turn, I unloaded the bag completely and spread all the remaining dogs and fries on the counter. Minutes later the counter was as empty as the parking lot. That was when I realized that cold sprinkly days were not great for the nursery business. The three of us chatted for a while in front of the portable electric heater, turning this way and that to get all our sides warm. That was when I learned that Caitlin used to work as a hairdresser and Bea used to raise bees and sell honey.

"Where did you have the bees?" Caitlin asked.

"Out in the desert by Vegas. Ain't the best place for bees. When it's hot, it's too hot, and when it's cold, the bees can't take that either. Then my girl ran away, up to the bay area. I left my old man and followed her to Gilroy. Been here about three years now."

"Did your daughter move here to be with her Grandma?" I asked.

"Heck no! Sugarbell, named after my husband's mother, only went to Aromas a couple times. She fell in with a bunch a kids livin' in Holiday Park. But they ain't kids no more."

"What do they do for a living...?" Caitlin asked.

"They pick up their food stamps...that's all I know." Bee's voice softened.

"Okay, ladies," I said, "I need to run an errand in town. See you later."

I let Solow out of the truck for a potty break, and then we cruised seven wet miles over to Holiday Park. I parked my pickup in the bike lane. Bea's poor little car looked so alone in that big field of wet grass. I pulled out my cell phone and punched in Barry's number, my insurance guy. Amazingly he answered on the second ring.

"Josephine, what can I do for you? Wrecked your truck again?"

"No, but I have a friend with a car that's stuck in the mud. Any idea how I can get it out?"

"Your friend should call...."

"She doesn't have towing insurance," I explained. "Is there any way she can borrow mine?"

Barry laughed. "You're kidding, right?"

"No, I'm not kidding. She can't afford a bumper, let alone a tow."

"We like to think we're charitable," he said. "Maybe I can pull a few strings. Give me the details and I'll see what I can do."

I gave Barry the dope, dropped my phone into a pocket and decided to look around while we waited for the tow truck. Still wearing rubber boots, even though the rain had stopped, I put Solow on leash and we followed Bea's tire tracks across the meadow toward the river. He pulled on the leash, nose just above the grass and mud as he ran along a barely-there double path of trampled grass. I loped along as fast as one can in cold wind, wet grass and sucky mud. The meadow started to slope down toward a narrow, shallow creek moving at a good clip. As we got closer to the water, I noticed pieces of clothing and a couple of blankets riding the river.

Solow began barking as we rounded a small grove of redwood trees. Up river about three hundred yards was an encampment of some sort being disassembled and rebuilt higher up on the bank.

My phone rang.

"Hello, Barry?"

"Yeah, it's me. I got a guy coming out there. Should be there in fifteen minutes."

"Thanks, Barry, I owe you...."

"Just do me a favor and stay out of trouble, Jo." He laughed, and hung up.

Solow pulled hard on the leash once the camp was in sight, but I was finally able to turn him around. With the wind at our backs, we made it back to my truck and climbed in. What a relief to be warm and comfortable. I thought about the people up river who were struggling to save their pathetic possessions. How cold and miserable they must be, I thought to myself as I watched a blue tent and dozens of tree branches float down the muddy river.

A yellow tow truck rumbled to a stop, window down.

I rolled my window down.

"Yours?" the driver pointed to the hatchback.

"Ah, yeah," I nodded, fingers crossed.

Our windows went up. The tow truck veered off the road as the driver expertly backed up over the curb. The big tires clawed their way across several yards of mucky meadowland and made a tight backwards turn that brought the truck back to back with Bea's car. I re-crossed my fingers, hoping her bumper wouldn't fall off. The beefy driver in overalls hooked up Bea's under-carriage and used his winch to yank the back of the car out of the mud and onto the hydraulic dolly system. Finally the car was strapped in position, ready to be towed.

Solow had grown tired of watching the poor man slopping around in sucky mud and fell asleep next to me.

I watched the tow truck driver climb into his seat and rev the engine. His tires spun as Bea's car waited quietly. The engine roared, and the tires dug deeper into the mud. The disgruntled driver climbed out of his seat, slammed the door and cussed at the filthy indolent tires. He pulled a shovel from his extra long toolbox, and be-gan digging and slinging mud, creating a clear path for his mucked-up tires. Finally, with sweat and raindrops running down his face, he climbed into the cab and fired up the engine. The tires spun. After many futile tries, the man called for help.

Over an hour later, a large yellow flatbed tow truck arrived.

My eyes were heavy, but I was determined to see Bea's car rescued.

The second driver conferred with the first, unhitched the little hatchback and latched onto the smaller tow truck. He lowered his platform and positioned it in front of truck number one. Everything on the second truck was bigger than on the first, including the winch that pulled number one truck up onto the platform. Number two driver revved his engine and his wheels crept for-ward an inch at a time.

My fingers hurt from the cold and from being crossed for such a long time.

The biggest truck slowly crawled out of the meadow and turned right onto Tiller. The rescued tow truck followed, hooked up at the side of the road like two love bugs in summer.

Number one tow truck was finally set free.

Number two tow truck driver drove away.

Number one tow driver rolled his window down.

I rolled mine down.

"Okay, lady, where do you want me to take this car?"

"To WildWest Nursery on Hecker Pass Road," I shouted.

He tipped his cap.

I was grateful that I had not been presented with a bill or anything to sign.

Good old Barry!

Chapter 13

Friday morning Jason handed me a nice paycheck plus some extra bonus cash when I arrived at the nursery ready for one more day of work before my well-earned weekend. He thanked me for buying lunch for his sister when he was away. I wondered why he didn't give Bea the cash so she could pay for her own lunch? Jason hinted that he wanted me to work at the nursery Saturday, but I held my ground, reiterating my policy of not working on weekends.

My mind bounced from Jason and Bea to visions of David and me spending quality time together, beginning with Friday dinner at Alicia's house in Watsonville. She said she was making tamales.

Solow slept while I trimmed a row of potted pomegranate trees, my back to the sun, wishing I were finishing the mural. But Jason needed me, so I proceeded down the row. Pomegranate barbs punctured my hands right through the gloves I wore. Swearing I would never eat another pomegranate, I left Solow in his comfortable hole-in-the-ground and strolled down to the gift shop for a band aid.

Remembering Thursday's tow truck trouble, and Bea actually thanking me for getting her car towed, I figured I had earned the right to ask her a few questions. I cornered her in the gift shop.

"Got a band aid? By the way, Bea, why don't you live with your brother in Aromas?"

"Cause my girl's in Gilroy. Here's a band aid." She handed me a white tin box with a red cross on the lid.

"Thanks." I opened the box. "You mean you live at the camp...?"

"If it's any ah yer business, I have a suite at the Hilton." She sucked on her cigarette and blew smoke in my face.

"You could live with your sister—Morgan Hill isn't far."

"You don't know my sister," Bea rolled her eyes.

"I watched you two fighting. She doesn't fight fair. Did she ever find the box of knitted stuff?" I asked, trying to keep the conversation going.

"No, but she thinks she knows who took it. Guess you better go sign fer them trees." Bea pointed to a large blue delivery truck entering the parking area. "Jason's in Hollister by now."

I moseyed out to the truck and greeted the driver, same truck and driver from two weeks ago. Same slick dresser wearing a man-bun.

"Hey, Ted, did you bring us more palm trees?"

The man stuck his head out the window. "Three more," he smiled, as he climbed down from the driver's seat and stretched his long arms straight up over his man-bun, then arched them out and down like a Sand hill Crane coming in for a landing. He sighed and asked where our restroom was located.

I directed Ted to the little room behind the gift shop that also shared a wall with the warehouse. From there, I went back to the parking lot to look at Ted's license plate. The metal plate holder said San Jose, but he had told me he drove up from Los Angeles. No big deal. The rest of the truck looked okay, so I went back to the gift shop to get warm.

Bea paced the shop nervously, shooting smoke out her nose. "What's he doin' in there, readin' the Sunset Guide to Everything?"

"I don't know," I said. "I just showed him where the restroom was. I'm going to the warehouse and sort bulbs." The first thing I saw when I entered the warehouse was Ted bent over pulling out and pushing in the half dozen drawers in an old metal chest full of sprinkler parts and pieces.

"Can I help you find something?"

Ted straightened up and turned to look at me standing in the doorway.

"Just wanted to see if old Jason has, ah, some of these sprinkler dealies."

"Which ones do you want?" I asked.

"Actually, I don't need 'em right away. I'll get 'em next time," he said, moving up the aisle, and back to the gift shop. As we stepped into the three-sided, colder-than-popsicles room, Ted tapped my hat with his hand. "Nice hat, where did you...?"

"Good Thrift Store," Bea spat. "I was with her."

Bea signed the papers for three palm trees, and I went back to the warehouse to count and package bulbs. I developed a program for keeping warm, fill ten bags of bulbs, and run up and down the aisle five times. Repeat as needed. Ten bags later, Bea walked into the room.

"What in a pig's holler are you doin?"

"Keeping warm," I panted. "Did Ted leave?"

"Yep, like a swarm ah bees was after him. Headed west on Hecker. I didn't know he delivered to Watsonville and there-bouts. Strange man, don't ya think?"

"He was acting strange, going through the drawers over there, looking for a sprinkler something-or-other," I said, as I finished my last run. My stomach growled. "Isn't it time for the food truck...?"

"Beep, Beep."

"Food truck's here," Bea announced.

"I'm on it," as Lito would say. I wrapped my scarf around my neck, collected my wallet and studied the menu printed on the side of the aromatic truck. Making an executive decision and flush with money for a change, I ordered food for Jason as well as Bea and myself which always included a few bites for Solow. Back at the shop, Solow sidled up to me, still dusty from the hole he had slept in. I rewarded him with a bit of chicken pulled from one of my tacos.

Jason arrived in time to enjoy paper plate Mexican cuisine. He saw the pink inventory sheet Bea had signed for three palm trees. With his mouth full of burrito, he said, "What's this?" He looked at Bea, as he waved the receipt in the air.

Bea drank her soda and blew smoke.

"That's from Ted..." I said, trying to be helpful.

"Obviously! But I didn't order three more palm trees from that creep. In fact, I didn't order the last load, but I didn't make a big deal out of it."

"He's up tah somethin,'" Bea said.

Jason turned, walked outside and slammed several carts into place.

A few customers found their way to the nursery, but not many. By two o'clock the boss told me to clock out. He and Bea could handle the workload for the rest of the day, which gave me time to primp and prepare for my dinner date with David.

That would have been the easy way to go. Instead, I loaded Solow into the truck, and we headed east on Hecker Pass Road to Lito's chocolate smoothie stucco house. Solow went with me to the door.

I knocked.

Solow howled.

Lito opened the door.

"Wow, that's quite a shiner you got there," I said.

"Yeah, I fell down the stairs. What are you doing out here, Josephine?"

"I was wondering if your dad's home…."

"Nope, he had to go to the office today. What's up?"

"If you're not busy, I thought we could check out some leads I have on Mrs. Oeblick's murder."

His face lit up. "I'm not busy. Let's go." Lito snagged a bulky blue jacket from the hall closet, helped Solow into the truck and climbed into the passenger seat. His size thirteen running shoes rested on the dog, and his knees pressed into his chin.

I backed up the truck ten yards to the street, cranked the wheel and soon we were cruising the highway toward Gilroy.

"Lito, who let your mom rent the cabin, Jason or his mother?"

"Jason. His mom was against it."

"Why was she against it?" I asked, checking the sky for rain clouds.

"I don't know why she hated my mom, but she did." He turned his head to stare out the side window.

"How did your mom feel towards Mrs. Oeblick?"

"Same. Where are we going?"

"I want to check on some people at the park. Do you mind?"

Lito laughed, "Sounds good to me. I like to get out whenever I can."

I wondered if he meant to say, "Whenever I can get away from my dad."

We roared down the road to the nearest burger place where I bought three hamburgers at the drive-up window. I handed one of them to Lito.

"Thanks, how did you know I was hungry?"

"I just followed the clues. You're young, male, and most likely hungry." A few minutes later, I parked my truck at the curb nearest the meadow where Bea's car had been stuck, hoping the ground had dried out. It hadn't. Lito, Solow and I trudged through sucky mud, heading toward the encampment off to the right, near the river. I tucked the bag containing two burgers and fries inside my jacket.

"Hey, look at that little guy," Lito said, pointing to something white and fluffy clinging to a log as it bobbed down river.

"Was that a little dog?" I gasped, one hand keeping the burger bag from slipping.

Solow had already veered to the left, leaving us behind as he raced toward the river. Lito and I had a hard time racing, but managed to plow across the mud at the speed of spilled paint. Lito reached the river just as the white fluff went by. He ran along the bank behind Solow, with me following several yards behind. As the river turned west, I lost sight of Solow, then Lito.

Solow howled in the distance.

Panting for air, I finally caught up to Lito. He stood at the edge of the river contemplating a dip into the dark frothy water where a couple of up-rooted olive trees were caught in a pile of branches and clutter that hadn't quite made it around the turn, but threatened to break loose at any moment.

"There he is!" I pointed to the right side of the pile-up, about twenty feet from shore.

"It looks deep...." Lito shivered.

"Here, hold the burger bag."

It took a moment for the cold water to penetrate my clothes and ignite my senses. It was all I could do to keep my eyes on the little dog as the choppy river slammed into the partially obstructed turn, roaring and churning. A ragged canvas folding chair raked my elbow and continued around the turn. Chest-high water gurgled and frothed around me as I waded toward the logjam.

Draped over a thick branch, the dog showed no sign of life. But I pressed on with Lito shouting directions over the roar, and Solow howling mournfully.

As if cold water lapping at my chin wasn't bad enough, the sky decided to open up and rain all over my parade. It didn't matter. I was already too cold and wet to care.

Someone's collection of recyclables floated by.

Finally I was close enough to the log to reach out and touch the soaking wet pooch. I couldn't decide if I felt any warmth or not. I began pulling the log behind me as I half swam, half walked to shore.

Lito reached out and snagged the log, pulling it the rest of the way up onto the grass. He reached out again and pulled me up to the grass where I fell on my knees, trying to catch my breath.

Little Dog was nearby.

I reached out and thought I felt something…or maybe not.

"Lito, hand me the bag."

"Huh? Oh, the bag?"

"Thanks," I sputtered, as I pulled the wrapper off a flattened burger and ripped off a piece of meat the size of a quarter. After waving the meat under the dog's nose for a couple minutes, the nose finally twitched. An ear wiggled. An eye opened.

Solow sniffed the little guy and licked him dry—as dry as one can be outdoors in the rain.

Little Dog was definitely interested in the burger but didn't have the strength to take a bite. Lito picked him up and shoved him under his jacket where he could benefit from the young man's body heat.

Without a word, we headed up-river to the camp where we hoped to find the owner of Little Dog.

Chapter 14

Steady raindrops finally thinned out until there were none. A piece of blue sky peeked through pregnant clouds. Grey river water rushed south as we headed north, Lito walking beside me with Little Dog inside his jacket.

Solow followed our deep footprints.

"Is Little Dog moving at all?" I asked, feeling cold and wet to my core.

"I can't feel anything. He only weighs about ten pounds," Lito said, as we came upon the first little pup tent, flap closed. Five tents later, a distressed blond in her early twenties approached us. Even in her distress, she automatically leaned forward and extended her hand for Solow to sniff.

"Have you seen a little white dog...?" she asked breathlessly.

Lito smiled and magically pulled Little Dog out of his jacket, like pulling a rabbit out of a cereal box.

"Oh my God, how did you...?" the young woman cried as she reached for her dear little friend. "Thank you...."

"Don't thank me. Josephine pulled him out of the river." Lito pointed his thumb at me and introduced us. "Where's your camp?"

Pointing down-river, she said, "My friend and I live in the first blue tent, except she hitched her way home when the rain didn't stop." She held the dog up to the side of her face. "My name is Sugarbell, and this is Vett."

At that point, Vett had both eyes open. His wet, matted fur had dried and turned into a mass of lovely white curls. He sniffed the air and looked at us, obviously feeling safe in Sugarbell's arms. Lito gave him a small piece of burger, which the dog chewed slowly and swallowed.

"Wow, Vett looks a lot like Jason's dog," I said to Lito.

"You know my uncle?" Sugarbell's blue eyes opened wide.

"If you're talking about Jason Oeblick...?"

"Yeah, he has Vett's brother, Charlie. He says I can live in his house in Gilroy once he gets it back from the witch—sorry, his ex-wife. But I might not go," she said thoughtfully. "I'm trying to make a difference here." She pushed a clump of damp, tangled hair away from her suntanned face.

"You mean this encampment?" I asked.

"Yeah, there are some troubled people here—some good, and some with bad habits. Mostly they've had hard luck, like me a couple of years ago."

"You can't save the whole world...." Lito said.

"No, but I might be able to help some of these people." Sugarbell pushed her face into Vett's soft fur. When she finally looked up, her eyes were moist. "There are several of us here who want to show the local government that we're useful. We keep our own tent areas clean, and we clean the park restrooms daily, three of them—all three are a long walk from here, in three different directions."

"You have to walk far to use a restroom?" I asked.

"Yep. They don't kick us out as long as we stay here on the outskirts of the park. This year has been rough with all this rain and the river coming up so fast."

"Yeah, we saw a lot of stuff going down the river," I said, searching the girl's face for traces of Bea. I didn't see any resemblance.

"Everybody moved their tents further back from the water, but a few nights ago the river rose again and some tents were lost. Very sad," she whispered, cuddling Vett under her chin.

"So, is it Vett as in Veterinarian?" Lito asked.

"No, Vett as in Corvette," she laughed. "His motor's always revved."

"May I ask what kind of hard luck brought you here...?" I asked.

"Family stuff. Sometimes you just have to leave," Sugarbell sighed.

"Would ya like something to eat?" Lito held up the flattened second hamburger.

Sugarbell smiled. "Sure, that's very nice of you. Where'd you get the shiner?"

"Ran into a door," Lito muttered.

Sugarbell gave him a sad, knowing smile as she unwrapped the burger.

I asked the young woman if she had been close to Mrs. Oeblick, her grandmother. Sugarbell shook her head and said that when she moved to California, she barely remembered the woman. She said she had only been to her grandparent's house once when she was five years old. She remembered being afraid of her grandmother.

"You haven't seen her since you grew up?"

"Once, for a family party," she said. Sugarbell stood beside her tent, silhouetted by a red ball of fire hanging low in the sky. I thought about the time, probably about four-thirty or five. Not much time to get home and ready for a dinner date with David.

"If we're out this way again, is there something we can bring you?" I asked.

"Well, the old lady in the tent next door to mine has arthritis in her lower back. She would love to have hot patches from the drug store. I'll pay you for them." Sugarbell walked with us past several tents and stopped in front of hers.

"You can't afford to pay me...."

"I have a job," she said, as she turned to enter her tent.

"They're on the house, Sugarbell." I flashed my hands up in the air. "We have to go now, but we'll be back."

"See yah around," Lito said, as we walked away.

Slogging forward through the mud and wet grass, my mind was stuck in the encampment with all those weather-beaten tents, shopping carts, blue tarps and second-hand possessions.

Lito asked me to take him to his mom's place because she had arranged to have him for the weekend, even though she would be working at the nursery Saturday.

I drove over the mountain to Watsonville and on to Aromas with Solow snoring and twitching on the floor and Lito scrunched up in the front seat like a bear in a phone booth. I dropped him in front of Jason's house, noticing the nosy neighbor across the street peeking out her window. I made a u-ey and drove down Otis to my house. Solow lay on the floor kicking the air with his hind legs. Was he struggling through sucky mud or chasing Fluffy? I would never know. All I knew was that it was almost six o'clock, and I looked like something dragged up from the river bottom.

A hot shower worked wonders at taking out the wrinkles in my favorite silk blouse, and the water felt great on my cold tired body. But I heard the doorbell ring and cut it short.

Solow howled his special howl just for David.

I laughed when I heard my fiancé talking to my dog as he patiently waited for me to dry my hair, apply lotion, mascara and lipstick. I exchanged my robe for the white silk blouse and a pair of black jeans, finishing off the ensemble with black boots, cranberry jacket and white silk scarf.

Decked out in Dockers and a dark brown leather jacket to match his eyes, David looked wonderful as usual. We quickly piled Solow into the back seat of David's Jeep and took off. It was a cloudless moonlit night and a bit chilly in the drafty vehicle. I zipped my jacket closed and shivered.

"Warm enough?" David asked.

"Compared to my day, this car is warm," I laughed.

David didn't ask about my day. He knew I was working on solving a murder mystery and preferred to distance himself from my shenanigans. I wanted to tell him all about Sugarbell and her little dog, but saved it for Alicia who was used to my detours from mundane life styles.

David parked the Jeep at our favorite Watsonville grocery store, and we hustled inside to buy a bottle of wine.

"David, what wine goes with tamales?"

My friend, Robert stepped up. "I know just the thing. Follow me." He proceeded to tell us all about his choice and why it went well with tamales.

"Thank you Robert," David said, taking the bottle to the checkout lane.

Robert walked along with me. "Anything new in the Oeblick murder?"

"Not really. It seems like everyone in the Oeblick family is pretty dysfunctional except for the gal I met today, Sugarbell, Mrs. Oeblick's granddaughter. She seems pretty normal—for a homeless person."

"Where have I heard that name?" he said to himself.

"Sugarbell seems nice enough but she lives in a little pup tent and wants to save all the homeless people. If she had a shower and clean clothes, she would look as good as any working woman. She seems smart enough and strong enough to support herself. I don't know why she didn't just move in with her grandmother for a while, until she got on her feet."

"Sounds like a strange family," Robert said, "I know where I saw that name. It was a story in one of those free newspapers, you know, local news."

"So why was she in the paper?"

"They were interviewing homeless people, and I remember Sugarbell because she had two years of college, in a nursing program, and seemed to be very level-headed. I wondered why she ended up in a tent." Robert turned to answer a call for "clean-up on aisle six."

Back at the Jeep, Solow sniffed the bottle of wine as if to say, "Where's the meat?"

"Sorry, Solow, no more burgers for you today," I said, climbing into the passenger seat. A few short minutes later, David parked the Jeep. We entered the Quintana house, where a fire crackled in the fireplace and the smell of hot tamales filled the air. Alicia graciously took the bottle of wine to the kitchen, and Ernie walked David over to a sofa facing the fire where they could discuss sports, world affairs and other manly topics.

Solow and Trigger's little dog, Tansey, romped from room to room until they needed a nap.

Helping Alicia in the kitchen was always fun for me, and I usually learned a few new cooking tips. My cooking needed all the tips that came my way. I sliced tomatoes and onions for the green salad while Alicia folded in a pound of shrimp and made the dressing from scratch. Spanish rice, tamales and refried beans were served family style.

Alicia and I were used to talking to each other while we worked on murals together. We hadn't worked together much in the last two weeks, so we had a lot of talking to catch up on.

"Jo, how was your day?" Alicia asked as she gathered five settings of silverware from the drawer and handed them to me.

"Wow, where do I start?" I said, placing forks, knives and spoons on the table. "I learned a lot today from a young woman in Gilroy. It seems Gilroy's homeless numbers have increased. But, of course, the problem is rampant all over the state. She said there are over five-thousand homeless people in Gilroy, and seventy-four percent of them are not in shelters."

"Who is this woman, and how does she come by this information?" Alicia asked.

"Her name is Sugarbell, she's homeless and she's been working with the city to get more people into shelters. She also helps out at the Compassion Center where people can get donated items they need...."

"Was she asking you for money?"

"No, she said she has a job and most of her neighbors get food stamps. Actually, she's more worried about the other people in the camp, like the lady next door with arthritis."

Alicia pulled hot tamales out of a large pot using a large slotted spoon, and placed them one-by-one on a platter. "Why doesn't her neighbor go to a shelter?"

"Because the shelters are first come, first serve. She would have to stand in line all day in the rain to get a cot."

"Jo, you can tell the boys dinner is ready."

I walked up to Ernie and David, who were bent over a newspaper in a political discussion, and informed them that dinner was on the table. Trigger had already washed his hands and took his seat. Tansey and Solow quickly positioned themselves under the table in case someone dropped a bite of food. I sat next to David, feeling like the luckiest girl in the world. I had a good man, a good dog, good friends and plenty of delicious food to eat. I wondered what Sugarbell would be eating for dinner.

"Jo, you're pretty quiet tonight—everything okay?" Ernie asked, as he uncorked the wine.

Alicia looked at her husband, "Honey, pour one for Jo, she needs to relax."

David laughed. "Careful what you wish for. Half a glass and she'll be asleep."

Ernie poured the wine, and then sat down in his chair. "David and I have been going back and forth on this homeless issue. The county wants to bring in these "little houses"—cheap and very basic. The county would even change building codes to get them in. This article also talked about a tent city. My fear is that if we make things too comfortable for these people, they won't think of it as temporary."

"But we can't just turn our heads and pretend they aren't cold and hungry," Alicia said.

"It's not a one-size fits all," David said. "Some people choose that life-style, but some are really down and out with bad luck, mental illness or addiction."

Alicia took a sip of wine. "What about someone like Sugarbell? She's educated and could be working, but she can't get cleaned up enough to go look for a good job."

"Yeah, how do you get hired when you look like you just fell off the turnip truck?" Ernie said.

"What do you think, Jo…?" Alicia asked.

Obviously everyone thought I couldn't drink without making a fool of myself. Silently vowing to show them, I sipped my half glass, and dosed off in a sitting position with my chin resting on my chest. Suddenly I heard my name.

"I'm sorry, what was the question?"

Chapter 15

Saturday morning arrived without songbirds or sunshine, just the steady pitter-patter of rain on the roof. A perfect morning to enjoy my warm bed, as my brain wandered through the events of Friday night. The Quintana dinner party was lovely, but the best was yet to come—time spent with David, driving home, being home, being in his arms. But the more comforts I experienced, the more I worried about Sugarbell living in the cold wet world of the homeless.

I had no specific plans for the day, just clean house and catch up on reading the mail and paying bills. Solow and I walked to the mailbox at the end of the driveway. Caitlin's truck rolled by with Lito at the wheel, apparently practicing for his driver's license. I waved, they waved and I collected the mail. Solow led me up the driveway to the house, keeping watch for scary white cats named Fluffy.

As I walked in the front door, I heard a message from the house phone.

"...and my stupid brother Rico's back in town. Call me."

I played the message from Bea again and jotted down her number. She said she had urgent news and wanted to see me in person right away. I called her, asked where we would meet and she said she was at Fern's house in Morgan Hill. She said she needed me to hurry over there.

Instantly my curiosity meter flew into the smokin' red zone.

Housework-be-darned, I poured kibble for Solow and hopped into my truck. If Bea and Fern couldn't stand each other, why was Bea there? And why did she sound out of breath? And why did she call me? With so much to think about, the miles quickly melted away. I exited the freeway at Cochran, zoomed through blocks of neighborhoods, roared up Hill Street and parked behind a hatchback with a red brick positioned behind the right back wheel—one brick that threatened to downgrade the whole neighborhood.

As misty showers dampened the eastern mountains, I stepped out of the truck, took in a breath of clean sweet air and looked across the valley. Living high above the Silicon Valley hustle and bustle might be nice, but not for me. I preferred ocean breezes, rolling hills and David living right next door. I would have no trouble leaving Hill Street to the rich and famous.

"Hey, Josephine, wipe that there goofy look off yer face and come over here!" Bea shouted from Fern's front door.

Couldn't she just say, "Thank you for coming"? I followed orders and marched over to a more disheveled-looking Bea than I'd ever seen before.

"Follow me," she demanded, and sped through the spacious home and down a flight of stairs leading to several more rooms. We passed through a large rumpus room, and hurried down a hallway that ended in a laundry room the size of my bedroom. Fern stood by the only window, where a shaggy-haired fellow was horizontally stuck, neither in nor out. His belly was inside the room while his butt was outside. The window frame seemed to be the problem as it rested on his lower back and refused to raise up no matter how hard the sisters pushed it.

"Okay, Josephine, ya know my sister, Fern, and this here is our other brother, Rico," Bea said.

Fern assured me that she had already notified the police, letting them know that the burglar alarm was a false alarm.

"So Fern and me decided we needed one more person. That would be you, so we can push, pull and pry all at the same time. Ya get the picture?"

I nodded.

Rico raised his head and groaned. "My legs are numb."

"And whose fault is that?" Fern snapped.

Bea cocked her head and squinted at her sister. "Maybe you could leave a stupid key outside somewhere so we could git in, yah think?"

"It's just like you, Bea, to blame me."

"Hey, you guys, shouldn't we get your brother out of the window before it rains?" I said.

"Yeah, before it rains," Rico said, lifting his head full of wavy black hair. He obviously hadn't had a haircut in the last six months, but he had beautiful brown skin and great bone structure. Half in the window and half out, it was hard to tell just how tall he was. I guessed he was at least six-feet.

"Okay, here's the plan," Bea said, picking up a crowbar and waving it toward the window like a pointer. "Fern's gonna pull on his arms while I pry the window, while you stand outside and push his feet. Oh, and Josephine, use this here door into the garage."

I did as I was told, pushed the garage door opener and stepped outside. A concrete sidewalk took me past three garbage cans and dead-ended outside the laundry room where two tired legs flailed madly.

"Josephine, grab his feet and push," Bea instructed.

"Rico, straighten your legs," I said.

He groaned, and lifted his legs up and out. I pulled well-worn huaraches off his bare feet, grabbed his arches and leaned into a hard push.

Through the window, I watched Fern grab her brother's wrists and pull back with all her strength, while Bea leveraged her crowbar between the window frame and the windowsill.

Fern had an idea. "We could pull his pants off and grease his bottom...."

"I'd rather die right here in the window," Rico said.

Bea shouted, "Flatten that perky butt of yours, little brother!"

"Don't you make fun of my brother's bottom...." Fern yelled.

"I won't make fun of Rico, if you start using those flabby arm muscles of yours."

"I don't have one inch of flab anywhere, unlike some people...."

"Who you callin' 'some people'?"

"Hey you guys!" I shouted. "On the count of three, give it all you've got."

"Ouch! Get that crowbar out of my rib!" Rico shouted.

"Sorry, little brother." Bea repositioned the heavy metal bar. "Next time use the door."

"I just got into town, I didn't know how to contact anyone. I was barely able to find the house, Morgan Hill has grown so much in ten years."

"Quit talking and suck in your stomach, Rico," Fern instructed, giving his arms another pull on the count of three. His body moved forward a few inches before the window frame stopped him. One more count to three, one more push and pull and he slipped into the laundry room like a salamander into its favorite pond.

When I made it back to the laundry room with Rico's shoes, Bea was leaning over her brother. Fern asked if he was all right, as he sat on the floor collecting himself. He pushed his feet into the shoes and stood up.

"You know my sisters?" Rico said.

"Yes, I'm working at the nursery, temporarily. Where do you work?"

Rico laughed. "Work is for peasants."

"What accent is that?" I asked.

"Portuguese," he smiled. "I'm Brazilian."

"As you can see," Bea said, "my little brother is fifty-two, six-foot-two and Latin-good-lookin.' There's plenty ah rich gals around, so he never has to work." She winked. "So when did you get in town, Rico, and why didn't you call?"

Rico scratched his head and smoothed his Bono t-shirt. "I lost my phone...."

"You can give us a better excuse than that," Bea quipped.

"Not really; you see I've been on the run from...."

"Are ya in trouble with the law?" Bea asked, her heavy eyebrows heading toward each other.

"No, nothing like that. It's a woman. She thinks we're getting married."

"Did you propose to her?" Fern asked, in a voice full of nails.

"No, she just got the wrong idea." He smiled, exposing straight white teeth.

Fern rolled her eyes.

Bea folded her arms. "So what else is new, little brother?"

Before Rico could answer Bea's question, I decided to leave.

"Nice meeting you, Rico," I said. "I think I'll be going now." I turned and walked through the garage and outside into partial sunshine. The neighborhood was steely quiet, not a soul around except for the gardener across the street clipping away at a deep green hedge. His white van had a ladder strapped to the roof and a brick in front of the left front tire. I always believed there was "someone" out there for everyone. Maybe this guy wearing a Giants baseball cap was for Bea.

Crossing the street was easy, no traffic in either direction. I walked up a concrete drive, turned left into the lawn area and stopped a couple feet from the gardener.

"Are you lost?" he asked.

"No, I just wanted to ask you one question since you have a perfect view of the house across the street."

He held his clippers in one hand at his side. "Ma'am, I just work here...."

"Did you happen to see a large cardboard box on the front porch a few days ago?" I pointed to Fern's house.

"No, even if I did, it's none of my business." He raised his clippers with both hands.

"Did you see someone take the box?"

"Maybc...why do you need to know?"

"I don't care one way or another, but Fern wants her mother's knitting stuff back. I guess she's sentimental about it."

"It was free pick-up day, you know, at the Good Thrift. They come around and take whatever you put out. I figured the box was there to be picked up and I guess Good Thrift thought so too." He began clipping the hedge.

"Thanks, you've been a big help." I hurried across the street and clambered into my truck. Zipping through Morgan Hill, I rolled up to the back entrance of the Good Thrift Store in record time. The first employee I found directed me inside to a wall of stacked boxes full of donated stuff ready to be examined, sorted and assigned shelf space in the store. So many cardboard boxes, so little time... only two guys sorting through boxes one at a time.

"Excuse me, would you mind looking in that box in the second row under the blue box?" I pointed to a box similar to the ones Bea had packed.

"Hey, Bud, can we do that?"

"Customers always right. I'll lift the blue one, you pull the box out."

Abbott and Costello pushed the box toward me. "There you go, ma'am."

I flipped the flaps open and looked inside at a large collection of women's shoes.

"Oh, sorry, this isn't the one," I said, closing the flaps.

Bud looked at Lou for guidance, then fearlessly pulled down a few more boxes. Number four box was a winner, full of knitted items and skeins of yarn. I was so excited I turned and hugged Abbott before he could get away. Costello was already entering the store when I shouted my thanks. I watched him smile and pocket my twenty-dollar bill.

Abbott loaded the box into the back of my truck and pulled the snug top down.

Something had nagged me about the box ever since it went missing. What was so important about knitted junk? Fern was a million miles away from being sentimental, and none of the family acted like they had cared a hill of beans about their deceased mother.

As soon as Abbott was gone, I opened the snug top, climbed up onto the back bumper, bent over the box and examined its contents thoroughly. Yep, it was knitted junk all right.

My stomach growled. I ran my hands along the bottom and sides of the box. "Nothing out of the ordinary here," I said to myself.

A young Good Thrift worker watched me shuffle through knitted hats, scarves and mittens. He cocked his head, hands in pockets. "Need some help?"

"No thank you. I'm just redistributing the weight."

I think he rolled his eyes, but I didn't care.

Fifteen minutes later, driving through Gilroy, I realized it was lunchtime and I was starving. I drove my truck into the take-out lane at my favorite hot dog place, spoke to a square of metal mesh embedded in a large menu board, and listened to the scratchy voice of someone inside the building. That someone told me to pay at the next window. Inching along behind a black pickup with oversized wheels and stinky exhaust, my turn finally arrived. I pulled to a stop at the window and turned to give money to....

"Sugarbell! What are you doing here?"

"I work here," she grinned. "How are you, Josephine?"

"Stunned, actually."

She leaned forward. "I have plans for the future."

"Good for you!" I said, as she handed over a bag of dogs and a drink.

Someone in a black BMW tooted a polite little toot-toot behind me.

"See ya later, Sugarbell."

The hot dogs were satisfying, but not as much fun as sharing dogs with Solow. Feeling satisfied on a food level, I decided to take the box of knitted stuff up to Fern's place, even though I would have to back-track a few miles to Morgan Hill. If she wasn't home, I planned to drop the box off at the nursery. As my truck powered up Hill Street, a blue delivery truck careened around a turn, too close for comfort. My wheel hit the curb for a second but I managed to get out of the bike lane, still growling at the truck driver.

Fern wasn't home but Rico was there. I gave the box to him.

"You want me to drop this at the Good Thrift?" he asked, looking puzzled.

"No, don't do that. Fern really, really wants this box."

"Don't worry, Josephine, I'll give it to her."

"Did she go back to work?" I asked.

"No, her boyfriend picked her up. You just missed her. It's starting to rain again, would you like to come in?" the spider said to the fly.

"Oh, thanks, Rico, but I have to get home. I have a big date with my fiancé tonight."

The front door closed.

I scurried across the damp lawn and climbed into my truck, knowing that grumpy Fern would soon be happily going through a box full of her mother's things. I tried to imagine Ms. Fashion wearing anything home-made or knitted—but the idea was completely unimaginable.

Chapter 16

Wanting to tell Bea about the box of knits, I decided to drop in at the nursery on my way home. I thought she would be happy, but getting Fern off her back wasn't enough. Something else was bothering her.

An old lady waddled into the gift shop carrying a severely wilted little plant still in its original black plastic pot.

"What can I do for ya?" Bea asked.

"I think it's sick," the woman said, holding up the eight-inch pot with her shaky freckled hands. She set the pot on the counter by the register.

"You bought that yesterday," Bea growled. "Did you give it too much water? I told you yesterday it don't like water."

The woman stared at a rusty drain in the center of the concrete floor.

"You people think you can kill plants and just come in here for a replacement. Ain't you ever had a business or even worked in one?"

"Relax, Bea, I'll take care of this. Ma'am, let's go for a walk."

The little lady followed me outside a short distance down the path. We stopped in front of a double row of nice green potted plants with large leaves resembling elephant ears. I explained to her that elephant ear plants love water, and she could drown them if she wanted to. She was thrilled. She said she had trouble remembering when she watered last, so she tended to overwater everything. I told her I had the opposite problem and tended to not water my marigolds at all. If it weren't for David, the poor things would have disappeared long ago.

Grumpy Bea exchanged the plants and gave the lady the two-dollar difference in price. If the little lady had been younger, she would have skipped out to the parking lot.

"What's wrong, Bea?"

"Do you see anyone else workin' here?" she snarked.

"Where's Caitlin and Jason?" I asked.

"Jason was clippin' the Japanese maples when he clipped his thumb right down to the bone. He ain't a fainter, but it looked like he was gonna keel over. I yelled for Caitlin and she came a runnin.' I wrapped a clean rag around it and Caitlin drove him to the doc...so here I am runnin' the whole shebang."

"I can help you out for a couple of hours, but I need to be home by five."

"That's mighty white of ya, Josephine."

I rolled my eyes and asked myself why I even bothered to help Bea. But she was like a clumsy old cow with a broken heart. Most people couldn't see her pain, just the grumpiness she hid behind. But I saw through it from day one.

Bea gave me a list of things to do, but first I had a couple of customers to wait on. When I finished ringing up a sack of redwood chips and three blueberry bushes, Bea had disappeared. A squashed cigarette lay on the floor next to a puddle of soda pop dripping out of a tipped over aluminum can. I stepped outside and scanned the rows of potted plants all the way to the eastern fence line. She wasn't there.

I rang up a shiny new red wheelbarrow for a gentleman, and watched him load it into his pickup, then scanned the grounds again. I checked the bathroom and the storage shed. Bea's disgraceful car was in the parking lot, but she was...."

I scratched my head, thought about ugly spiders and suddenly knew where I should look. As I ran down the path to the tool shed, I remembered Bea's crabby attitude. But that didn't slow me down. I pulled the metal door open and looked inside. It took a moment for my eyes to adjust, but I heard hiccupy sobs.

"Shut the door, it's cold out there," Bea croaked.

"You'd rather be in there with the spiders?"

"Ain't no spiders...go away, Josephine."

A young couple—prospective customers, were coming closer so I quickly closed the shed door. They were looking for a willow tree for their front lawn. I followed them, reading labels as I went. Fortunately, they spotted the type of tree they wanted. I supplied them with a flatbed cart, hefted the gangly seven-foot tree onto it and rolled it over to the gift shop. I rang up the tree and checked my watch. Four-thirty already! I started to walk away.

"You can load the tree into that blue pickup over there," Ms. Customer said, as Mr. Customer fumbled around putting his credit card neatly back into his manly wallet that matched his belt and shoes exactly. I put the tailgate down, climbed up onto the flatbed cart, lifted the tree and slid it into the bed—secretly hoping it would fall over at the first bump in the road. I slammed the tailgate shut and walked away, heading toward the shed as the winter sun disappeared behind the mountains and shadows deepened.

"Bea?"

No answer.

"Bea, I'm coming in." I opened the door and looked around. She sat on an up-side-down bucket, her chin resting on her chest.

"What's going on with you...?"

"I don't feel like havin' a little chitty chat with you, okay?"

"I understand how irritating customers can be...."

"Not customers, life!" Bea said, wrapping her arms around her mid-section.

"How can I help...."

"Ya can't." She rocked back and forth for several minutes while I tried to think of a way to get her ugly mood out of that ugly shed. Every couple minutes I stuck my head out the door to see if any new customers were on the grounds.

The automatic outdoor lighting kicked in, illuminating much of the nursery.

"Bea, did you know that I lost my husband seventeen years ago when he was run over by an eighteen wheeler?"

"Of course I didn't know. You think I'm one a them psychic dopes?"

"I'm just saying, I've been through some hard times, and I'd like to help you with yours."

"My hard times started early," she growled. "One minute I'm a happy four-year-old, next minute my last name is Oeblick. I got a brother, Jason, and a sister named Fern. Four years later, we all go on a trip and snatch a boy named Rico. My 'parents' think they're helping to alleviate poverty by redistributing the child population. That's the way Dad put it. In reality, we were their new little slaves."

"Oh, Bea, that's awful...."

"Then it gets worse. Fern's skinny cause she refuses to eat, Jason takes up cowboyin', hopin' he'll go out of this world in glory, and I run away and hook up with a no-good loser. Useless Rico seems to have found a good life. But I'm not sure cause I've only seen him twice in the last thirty-five years."

Everything Bea said was shocking, sort of. But some of it I had already seen for myself. The first time I met Jason, Fern and Bea, I had the impression they were not a close family. I watched Bea straighten her back, lift her chin and wipe her eyes. She stood up and marched past me, straight to the gift shop and through it to the restroom.

While standing outside the shop wondering if Bea was going to be okay, I pulled out my phone and called David. He had planned to pick me up at six for dinner and a movie. I told him I needed more time, and he agreed to pick me up at seven for dinner and a later movie. I helped Bea close up the nursery at six and made it home by six forty-five.

Home at last. All I had to do was feed Solow, run a brush through my hair and put together a ravishingly beautiful outfit to wear. Short of that, I pulled on a clean pair of black jeans and a peach color sweater. Black three-inch boots and a rather dated silver jacket completed the ensemble. The doorbell rang as I touched up my lipstick. And then I remembered I hadn't eaten in a very long time.

Solow welcomed David at the front door, and I welcomed him in the kitchen. He said I looked lovely. I thought he looked drop-dead gorgeous. But my strongest feeling was hunger, so I quickly ushered him out of the house and into the car. David fired up the Miata's engine and backed the car onto Otis.

Caitlin's pickup truck squealed to a stop behind us. Lito was driving—alone.

"That's odd," I said, "Lito's driving by himself. I wonder if he has his license now." We rolled into Aromas with Lito right behind us. David curbed the car in front of The Aromas Grill, and Lito parked behind us. As we walked inside, Lito caught up to us and sat down at our table.

"I'm so hungry," Lito said. "Don't worry, I brought money. My dad gives me money—says I should eat a lot while I'm still growing. He wants me to be tall."

"I think you're tall already," I said, thinking about Caitlin's sparsely filled fridge and wondering how Lito could survive, let alone grow taller.

"Are you with your Mom for the weekend?" I asked.

He nodded absently as he read the menu.

"I heard that Jason had an accident...."

"Yeah, but Mom took care of it. Got him to the doctor real fast. She stayed with him and didn't get home until a few minutes ago. She said she wanted me to have a good dinner and bring something back to her. She likes the salmon here. I'll surprise her with that."

"Why didn't Caitlin come with you?"

"She was too tired. She's been working long hours lately." Lito smiled at something on the menu and looked no further. "How's the mural coming along?"

"I'm waiting for better weather," I said, still scanning my menu.

"Do you need help with it?" Lito asked.

"Ah, sure. I can find work for you. I'll let you know the next time I paint."

A perky young waitress asked if we were ready to order.

I ordered deep-fried mushrooms because I was so hungry and didn't think I could wait for the entree. Lito and I dove into the crispy little mushrooms with zeal while David sipped a frothy beer. Responding to a few casual questions, Lito told us about his parent's breakup, how his dad was recovering from brain surgery and refused to take his medicine. He had lost his job months ago and began a career based on staying home doing nothing while Caitlin worked two jobs and Lito made pizzas at the pizzeria instead of going off to college.

"Do you get along with your dad?" I asked, as our meals were served.

"Yeah, I guess so. He used to have a lot of head-aches, so I stayed out of his way most of the time. But he has a job now, and he seems happy to have me around," Lito laughed, making light of a serious situation. "Mom's making house payments plus paying rent money to Jason."

"Doesn't your dad know how his behavior's affecting you and Caitlin?"

"I don't know…but I think he's trying."

The waitress leaned in and asked Lito if everything was okay.

David's eyebrows went up, and I couldn't help smiling as Lito asked for extra napkins. The girl looked back at him once as she walked back to the kitchen.

"What's her name?" I asked.

"Who? Oh, her…that's Katie. She was in my Spanish class…in Gilroy."

Halfway through our meal, Lito's phone rang. He stopped eating and held the phone to his ear. "Slow down, Sugarbell, and tell me where you are."

I automatically leaned closer to Lito and listened to the frantic voice on the other end.

"You're on Tiller Street at the kid's park by the restrooms, got it."

Lito waved to Katie who just happened to be looking at him from across the room. She followed his instructions and quickly boxed up his leftover ribs and the salmon salad he had ordered for his mother. As he pulled out his wallet, David waved him on.

"You're in a hurry," David said." I'll take care of it. Go." He flicked his hand toward the door. Lito grabbed the boxes and scurried outside. We heard Caitlin's truck peel out and roar down the street. I crossed my fingers, hoping he had an actual driver's license.

Ten minutes later, David asked if I still wanted to go to a movie.

"What if we go to a movie in Morgan Hill and pass through Holiday Park on the way."

"I figured as much," he said, trying to hide his smile. "You're worried about the boy, or is it Sugarbell you're worried about?"

"Yes, and yes." I led the way to the car. The stars were out and the love of my life was driving me to a homeless encampment, of all places.

"If this Sugarbell girl is homeless, even though she has close relatives all around this area, how and why does she call Lito?" he asked, as we headed over the mountain to Gilroy.

"Maybe Sugarbell doesn't want to bother her family? She has a job and a cell phone and she's trying to help all those homeless people. I'm not sure why she called Lito. I think Fern or Jason would help her, and even give her a place to stay. But she feels she can't advocate for the homeless unless she's one of them. The poor old lady in the tent next to her is crippled up, and there's a young veteran up the way who lost his leg. Sugarbell said he was too depressed to go through the government hoops to get help."

"I have a lawyer friend, retired, belongs to my golf club and I bet he could help this veteran," David said.

"Wouldn't that be wonderful...." I cooed.

"Yeah, I'll look him up. I haven't seen him in a couple years."

"That gives me an idea. I bet there are other people in your golf club who are talented in one way or another. Like a doctor, lawyer, teacher...you know, people who could volunteer a little time to get these people on their feet. At least the homeless who are willing to try." I said, thinking out loud.

"I noticed Veggout is looking for workers," David said. "One volunteer driver could deliver four or five workers...."

"But," I said thoughtfully, "how do these people clean up and dress for an interview?"

"How does Sugarbell do it?" he asked, as we turned onto Tiller.

"I don't know exactly, all I know is she's young, strong and determined."

David sniffed. "I smell smoke."

"I smell it too. What's that glow...?"

Chapter 17

I was so focused on a red glow in the dark sky ahead of us, that I almost missed seeing a little white dog trotting along Tiller Road.

David parked the car and climbed out, his hair fluffed in the breeze.

I leaped out of the car, scaring Vett into a run. He slowed to a walk, but each time I approached him, he ran a few yards away from me. It was eight o'clock on a moonless winter evening and colder than an alpine icicle. Finally, I squatted down on my heels and let Vett come to me. Once I had him in my arms, I felt the warmth of his active little body.

"Josie, I'm going over there and see what's making that red glow...."

"I'm right behind you," I said, my heels sinking into the moist earth with each gooshy step. Breathing in smoky air a couple of yards behind David, I could barely see him as we cut across a lumpy field. Vett bounced in my arms. The burnt wood smell became stronger. I tried to think of bonfires at the beach with hot dogs, marshmallows and waves crashing against the sandy shore. Instead, we heard a fire engine pumping water and the sizzling sound of cold water hitting hot pine needles.

"Maybe Lito and Sugarbell are over there, behind the fire trucks," I said.

"Maybe, let's go." David's long easy strides were hard to keep up with, but I was determined to see if my friends were in the area. The sizzling continued as white smoke billowed and then dissolved into blackness, gobbling up the red glow.

"Is that you, Josephine?"

Vett squirmed.

I turned around.

"Oh my God, you found my little Vettie!" Sugarbell cried, as she took him into her arms. "How did you find him? I've been looking for him for a couple hours. I even called Lito to help me. Thank you, Josephine, I'm so happy."

Lito stepped into the light from the trucks.

"You found the dog. That's great."

"Yeah, but what happened here?"

Sugarbell adjusted the dog in her arms. "It all started when two homeless guys found a pack of cigarettes in the trash. The younger of the two took off with the whole pack, so the older guy set fire to the young man's shopping cart full of belongings. Unfortunately, the cart was parked under this pine tree. When I called the fire department, it was for the cart. When they got here the tree was on fire."

"Was anyone arrested?" David asked.

"Not yet, but this fire won't help our case with the city. We're trying to show how law-abiding we are, and then this happens," Sugarbell lamented. "The younger man's cart had a stack of newspapers in it. As you can imagine, the ash floated right up into the tree."

"Newspapers?" David said.

"Yeah, I happen to know he's a crossword puzzle expert."

"What a waste of talent," I mumbled.

"We have many talented people in our group, like George, the out-of-work plumber. He keeps the park restrooms in good shape. And Doris, she makes delicious soup for the camp out of whatever scraps people give her. But, of course, she can't cook in the rain."

"Sounds like a nice little community...." I shivered and zipped up my jacket.

"We try, but when the hoods come along and put graffiti everywhere, we get blamed," Sugarbell said. She adjusted the striped blanket draped over her shoulders while holding Vett steady.

Lito stepped behind her and arranged the blanket to cover the back of her neck. "Hey, I gotta get home before Mom has a hissy. See ya later," he said as he turned and walked back to his mother's truck.

With the fire out, the air had become colder and darker.

"Would you like to come down to the camp and meet some people?" Sugarbell asked.

David said he would like to go there, and I said, "Thanks for inviting us." Easier said than done; the three of us, plus Vett, stumbled across the lumpy field bumping into each other in the dark and laughing at nothing in particular. We finally arrived at the camp that used to be closer to the river but now was situated about twenty feet from the water and sheltered by a stretch of young redwood trees.

Sugarbell turned on a battery-powered lantern and brought out two heavy blankets from her tent. David and I sat on a wooden apple box and shared a blanket. Sugarbell had her own box and blanket. All we needed was someone to tell a spooky story, but no one spoke for a while. We just listened to the noises coming from various tents, like coughing, laughing, crying and even someone singing. Whoever it was, he sang "Blue Tail Fly."

"Jimmy Crack Corn and I Don't Care," wafted down the line of tents, entertaining us briefly. I felt relaxed even though the box was hard as a rock to sit on and my body craved warmth.

Vett fell asleep on Sugarbell's lap.

Suddenly a couple of snorts and a long snore came from close by—from Sugarbell's tent, actually. Vett didn't even wake up, but David and I automatically turned our heads, following the snoring sounds.

"Sorry, I didn't know Mom was in the tent...."

"It's getting late," I said. "We should go."

"It's just Bea in there," she explained.

"We should go. She probably came to see you...."

"No, she lives here." Sugarbell smiled. "I'm the visitor."

I leaned closer to her. "Bea had a hard day today," I whispered.

"Yeah, she has a lot of those."

"What do you think is wrong?" I whispered, "Is there something I can do to help?"

"It's depression and she's off her meds. She thinks we can't afford them. I keep telling her we can, but she can't think straight when she's like this. Sooner or later I'll get her to take her medicine, but she might have to hit 'bottom' first."

I wondered if a person off their meds could kill another person.

David stood up. "Thanks, Sugarbell; enjoyed meeting you."

She smiled at David and turned to me. "Oh, by the way, Josephine, I'm in charge of a five-mile run through Gilroy to help raise money for the homeless projects around here. Can I sign you up?"

"Do I look like a runner?" I asked, hoping Sugarbell would think I was over the hill age-wise. But I guess full-figured fifty-year-old women were encouraged to run. With no cordial way out, I signed on the bottom line with the pen she just happened to pull out of her pocket. She handed me several pages of paperwork to take home and complete, and encouraged me to get out and sign up sponsors. In other words, beg for money.

"Exactly when is this race?" David asked, looking interested.

Sugarbell handed him a set of paperwork. "The run is next weekend...."

"Not much time to get in shape," he laughed.

"You look like you're in fine shape," she said, with goo-goo eyes. Good thing David was fifty-five and she was very, very young, or I would have had to put her in her place. Just because I wasn't in a hurry to marry him didn't mean I didn't love him. I couldn't imagine myself without David.

On the way home, we chatted about the upcoming run. Neither one of us had ever done anything like that before. In the past I had told myself that I would like to try running with a pack of people for some good cause—it always looked like fun on TV. Now that it was actually going to happen, I had doubts and questions. David answered them to the best of his knowledge, as a first time runner himself.

Our plans to see a movie were long forgotten. It was ten o'clock, I was sleepy, and David and I had planned to skip Church and go to an early breakfast at the Aromas Grange the next morning. His little Miata ate up the miles as we discussed the fire, the camp and the run. We turned onto Otis and were almost home when sirens wailed in the distance. They became louder, as they headed our way.

David pulled the car to the side of the road, two right wheels in a ditch and oak branches scraping the roof.

Red and Blue swirly lights passed us and headed up Otis Road.

We followed the sheriff's car as far as my driveway, where I asked David to please follow the lights and see what the emergency was. He consented, despite his better judgment, but drove slowly, carefully, while I leaned into the windshield straining to see what might be around the next turn as I white-knuckled the door handle.

David pulled into Jason's driveway and parked behind the sheriff's cruiser. We piled out of the car and walked toward the house. The front door was open and we heard voices. But it wasn't any of our business, so I suggested we check on Caitlin and Lito to see if they were all right.

Leaping out of the car, I veered left across the lawn and ended up at the cottage.

David followed at a more dignified pace.

The lights were on so I knocked on the door. The lock clicked and the door opened.

"Hey, Josephine, what are you doing out here at night?" Lito asked.

"We heard sirens and wanted to make sure you and your mother were okay," I said.

"We're fine," he turned to look at his mom.

Caitlin walked up and stood beside Lito. "We called the Sheriff because we saw lights and heard noises in the big house, and Jason won't be home until tomorrow."

"Wow, wonder what's going on...." My heart sped up a notch.

Lito said, "We heard a car drive up to the big house about an hour ago and then it left. A little bit later, we heard glass breaking, and then the lights came on. Someone broke into that house," he said. "I wanted to go see who it was but Mom wouldn't let me."

"It's cold out there," Caitlin said. "Come in and get warm."

David made himself comfortable on the couch but I stayed by the window, glancing outside every couple minutes to see if anything was happening. After what seemed like an hour, we finally heard car doors slam and the cruiser rolled down the driveway. The taillights disappeared a moment after I let myself out Caitlin's front door, into the cold dark night. I shivered as I walked swiftly across the lawn and up the path to the front door.

"Josephine, wait a minute!" David shouted.

I slowed my walk, eyes still focused on light coming from the front room windows. The Sheriff's deputies hadn't bothered to let us know what the situation was, but I figured no one had been arrested since the lights were still on. Someone must be in the house.

David caught up to me as I knocked on the door.

We heard footsteps. The door opened and Rico peeked out.

"Wow, Josephine. I thought maybe those snoopy cops were back," he laughed. "And who's that?" he pointed to Lito and Caitlin coming up the walk behind us.

After quick introductions, Rico asked us to come inside. He looked like he had just arrived from a very warm climate, wearing white cotton slacks, a white short-sleeve button-up shirt and huaraches with no socks. He was probably much colder than we were in our jackets. A black cloth backpack sat on the floor. Rico quickly scooped up the blankets he had arranged on the couch, taking the bundle into the next room.

"Sorry, this is my bed tonight. Have a seat." He pointed to the leather couch and we all sat down, elbow to elbow.

"Did you forget to call Jason...?" I asked, holding back my grin.

"I called the house phone and no one answered. I figured he was busy or sleeping."

"Your family ties are a bit sketchy...." I said.

"You could say that. My girl friend is visiting her folks in Willow Glen, so I thought I'd pop in and see my own family. So far it hasn't been as easy as it sounded. I met her family, left her there with her mother and got an Uber ride to Aromas, I mean, ah, Morgan Hill. Had a little trouble getting into Fern's house...."

I laughed. "Big trouble getting into her house."

"That's funny," Lito said. "You say this is your first visit to Aromas?"

"Yeah, I was busy...." Rico muttered.

"I thought I saw you weeks ago at the Halloween party the day Mrs. Oeblick died," Lito said, eyes trained on the perfectly tanned and red-faced lady-killer. "Must have been someone else I saw."

"No one else looks like Rico," I blurted.

Rico smiled smugly, taking my words as a familiar compliment.

"No one else wears lightweight, all-white clothing in the middle of winter. You would be easy to spot," Lito said. "Of course, it was a costume party—mostly pirates, but only one pirate wore huaraches."

"Hey, Pal, don't worry about it," David said to Rico, standing up to leave.

I reluctantly followed him to the car, climbed in and he closed my door.

"Didn't you believe what Lito said he saw?" I asked.

"Maybe, but how can you prove it. The more you two badgered him, the more defensive he got. He's only human."

"Well, David, I didn't think you were paying attention. And you're right, now that we know Rico was there, we just have to prove it. Maybe Uber can help us."

"You look like you need some sleep, Josie."

He kissed me under the porch light and opened the front door for me. I entered, but he didn't follow.

As tired as I was, I tossed and turned in my bed for almost an hour. Did I really tell the Good Thrift people that Bea was off her meds? I never would have said such a thing if I had known it was the truth. I think my face turned red in the dark.

Finally I drifted off into a nightmare. In the mist, I saw Rico creeping along Jason's roofline like a cougar after its prey. I wanted to warn Jason and his mother, but my hands and feet were tied to a tree and no sound would come out of my mouth. I watched Solow trot over to the front door where Mrs. Oeblick invited him in and then shut the door. I was alone except for a family of owls on a branch above my head. There were noises coming from the house. I looked up as Solow, Lito, Rico, Daphne, Fern and Jason all ran out the door.

Mrs. Oeblick did not come out.

Chapter 18

Sunday morning, I lay in bed analyzing my latest nightmare. Was there an actual clue in the scary jumble of the dream? In my nightmare, Lito, Rico, Daphne, Fern and Jason had unified as the co-murderers of Mrs. Oeblick. They all looked guilty of murder. But in the light of day, Rico was the only one I truly suspected— unless Lito was lying for some reason. Bea might have committed murder in a fit of blind depression, or Mrs. Oeblick's ex-husband's girlfriend Daphne could have done it in a fit of meanness. But I didn't seriously think of them as murderers, just weird people.

I checked the time. Wow, David would be picking me up in half an hour. The shower was short, the dressing quick and the coffee was only two sips.

Tapping on the front door and a long howl from Solow let me know that my knight in Levis and navy blue pea jacket had arrived.

We embraced.

"Cold out there," he said, rubbing his palms together.

Our eyes met as the same thought grabbed each of us and wouldn't let go. How were the homeless going to keep warm? David's smile faded along with mine. Pulling on my warmest coat, I wished I had never seen the plight of the homeless.

"Are you looking forward to the race next Sunday?" I asked David.

"I'm going to force myself to play eighteen holes of golf everyday this week to get in shape." A sinister grin spread across his handsome face.

"I'm thinking of running everyday on my lunch break," I said.

We said goodbye to Solow, and David drove us one mile to Aromas.

"We should have jogged into town," David said, as he parked his car at the Aromas Community Grange.

"Are you kidding? Think of all the hills we would have to run up. I don't mind running down, but I hate running up. And speaking of running, look who just entered the building."

David turned to look. "Hey, it's Rico. Looks like he ran all the way from Jason's house."

"But now he's all sweaty...." I said, wrinkling my nose. And who's that guy walking in behind him? Isn't he one of your golf buddies?"

"Yep. I'll talk to him about helping the veteran Sugarbell told you about."

The golf buddy and Rico queued up behind us. Several people were ahead of us in line, moving slowly toward the volunteer purveyors of breakfast. Standing in line wasn't bad. Jesse, a local musician, strummed his guitar and sang, folks mingled and bacon sizzled. Home of fifteen different leagues, clubs, guilds and foundations, the one-hundred-year-old grange building hummed with music and conversation.

Long tables meant sitting with old friends and new. Balancing fully loaded plates, David and I slithered into empty chairs directly across from Rico and the golf buddy, whom David introduced to me as "Slicer."

"Nice to meet you, Slicer. Does your nick-name come from work or golf?" I asked, as I arranged my full plate and silverware.

A volunteer came around and poured coffee for us.

David laughed, "Both."

Slicer nodded and introduced the sweaty guy next to him.

"We know Rico," David said. "How's it goin,' Rico?"

Rico chewed on a piece of sausage, swallowed and finally answered. "Great, just like old times. I used to come here when I was a hungry teenager. I'd sneak out of the house and run down here. They always gave me food."

"Where's your gal?" Slicer winked.

"She's visiting her family," Rico said, as his eyes followed a shapely young woman across the room pouring coffee refills.

I was dying to ask Slicer how he knew Rico, but David had already started a conversation concerning homeless veterans. I didn't want to stop them, so I waited, and waited and waited. Golf and retirement were added to the conversation, and I continued to wait for the right time to ask my question.

Rico excused himself and left.

Slicer said he had a tee time in half an hour and stood up to leave.

"Slicer, before you go," I said, "how do you know Rico?"

He frowned as if I'd asked for something confidential—probably a holdover from his work ethics.

"Actually, we met right here...."

"But this breakfast only happens once a month," I said.

"Yeah, about a month ago. Nice guy, that Rico. He was with his mother."

Pins and needles ran up and down my body. I watched Slicer leave, and turned to David, "Did you hear that?"

"Yeah, they met right here at the grange. What's the big deal?"

"The big deal is Rico lied and told me he hadn't been to see his mother in Aromas. Mrs. Oeblick was still alive Sunday morning, and she had her last breakfast right here at the grange." Suddenly my stomach felt queasy. "Let's go home."

"All of a sudden you want to go...oh, I get it, you want to...."

"Shhhh!" I said. "Not that. I want to give Rico a lift. Maybe he's tired after all that running and eating."

"And maybe you can pump him for information about his mother's murder," David said, as I pulled him across the parking lot to his car. He fiddled with his keys and checked the mirrors.

I sent a noisy puff of air out between my lips.

Finally David turned the key, dropped the shifter into reverse and backed up slowly like a very old lady with her mind on her latest knitting project. Rico was halfway to Jason's house when we finally stopped to offer him a ride. At first he refused.

"Rico, did you know you can have a heart attack from too much running?" I said. "If you sweat out all your minerals, your heart can't...."

"Okay, I'll go with you."

I climbed out of my seat so that Rico could climb into a back seat created for very small people. It took some time for him to settle in, with his knees against his chest. I climbed back in and off we went.

"So Rico," I said. "I'm glad you had some time with your mother the day she died."

David shot an eyeball "What are you thinking?" dagger my way.

Rico looked at his knees. "Yeah, I didn't tell anyone because I'm on parole. I'm not supposed to leave Santa

Clara County. But I really wanted to see my mom, see if she was still as mean as I remembered."

"Was she?" I asked.

"Actually, she had mellowed a bit."

"Was she mean to everyone?" I asked, as David's face contorted.

"She was mean to everyone except Fern, dear old Fern, her favorite child." Rico rolled his eyes and sighed. "She let Fern buy the homestead for a song, no surprise there."

"Did you know that Fern plans to sell it to your dad?"

Rico's jaw dropped. "Nobody told me that. If that's true, then good for Dad."

David drove to the end of Otis, and dropped Rico in front of Jason's mailbox.

I glanced across the street. The drapes closed.

David turned the car around and sped down the road to my house. His jaw finally relaxed. There would be no more gossip about the Oeblick family. He hated gossip. David walked me into my house, we hugged good-bye and kissed goodbye again and again. An hour later, David left, promising to be back in seven hours to take me to dinner at Alicia's. The usual Friday night dinner had been canceled because Trigger was down with a cold and Alicia didn't want us to catch it. Saturday she decided he was not contagious anymore and invited David and me to Sunday dinner.

Thinking ahead, I realized that four days from Sunday, it would be Thanksgiving Day; and I still didn't know where I would be celebrating. Mom and Dad were tinkering with the idea of having it at their house, and David thought he might have it at his place.

The homeless race loomed, and I was out of shape. I decided to practice running up and down Otis and stop at all the neighbors to collect donations as I went.

The weather had finally turned a corner. The cold wind had blown away and sunshine ruled the day. I stuffed a folded sign-up sheet into my Levi pocket, traded my heavy coat for a windbreaker, traded heeled boots for tennis shoes and set out for a quick run with Solow. Most of my neighbors were not home. The first one who answered her door was obviously north of eighty so I just asked for a small donation for the homeless. The second person to answer a door was a young man fresh out of the shower. He smelled like Irish Spring and kept a tight hold on his wrap-around towel as he awkwardly signed his name on the sign-up sheet.

My last stop was a two-story house perched at the top of a knoll, directly across the street from Jason's house. The foresty, gated acres had a sign out front that read, "Locked and Loaded." But I was not discouraged. I ignored the sign, climbed the metal rail fence and Solow squeezed under it. We bravely walked up to the porch, and I rang the doorbell. Out of the corner of my eye, I saw the drapes move in the window off to my left. Then came heavy footsteps.

The front door opened. A tall sturdy, built like a rusty tank, lady in her sixties peeked out.

"I'm not buying anything today," she said as she tried to push the door closed. But my foot happened to be in the way.

"Hi, my name is Josephine, actually I'm your neighbor—sort of. I live down the street," I said, pointing toward home.

"How'd you get in here?" she asked, raw sienna eyes squinty, large puffy hands ready to slam the door in my face.

"I'm sure you've heard about the homeless problem...."

"I don't see any homeless." She spread her fingers wide and cocked her head full of straight bronze but going grey hair. "Do you?"

"The people I'm trying to raise money for are in Gilroy. Did you know that there are over five thousand homeless over there? Many of them are sick and unable to work."

"Santa Cruz has that number beat..." she snarked.

"It's a problem everywhere, but we have to start somewhere. Would you like to sign up for a runathon to raise money—you can walk if you want to...."

"Maybe I could just bounce," she laughed. "I feel for those people, really I do, but can you honestly see me running down the road?" She patted one large hip, laughed and finally took her hand off the doorknob so she could stroke Solow's velvety ears. "Nice dog, what's his name?"

"Solow."

"Whom do I write the check to?"

I quickly scanned the sign up sheet. "Write it to 'The Homeless Fund'."

The woman disappeared inside the house for a couple of minutes and came back with a check for five-hundred dollars. I was beyond speechless. I thanked her several times. Solow and I hurried out the gate before she could change her mind.

We were quite ready to be home after a couple of hours prowling the neighborhood. I had spent more time knocking on doors than actual running, but I figured I would get my exercise during the week. And I planned to eat lightly on turkey day. A little weight loss couldn't hurt. My fantasy was to look like a tall lanky runner bursting through the finish-line ribbon as the crowd cheers.

Solow and I entered my house. I flopped down on the couch, and he curled up at my feet. I stared at the check, feeling like it was too good to be true. The name on the check was Molly Pearson. Searching my pockets for the sign-up sheet, I finally remembered setting it down on Molly's porch railing. I had managed to get four names on the sign-up sheet, and I needed to get it back. I still had two hours left before David would pick me up for our dinner at Alicia's, and it wouldn't be dark for another hour. And I would get more practice running.

Solow showed no interest in another walk, so I took off alone. I jogged west on Otis, slowing to a walk on the uphill climbs and speeding up on the downhill. A dog barked in the distance and an owl hooted from a tree at the side of the road. My windbreaker failed to keep me warm, but I kept going because I was beyond the halfway point. When I finally reached Molly's gate, I didn't have enough wind left to spit let alone speak so I climbed over the fence and knocked on the door.

Molly poked her head out. "I thought you'd be back," she laughed. "I see you signed up Lito, across the street. Seems like a nice boy."

"Yes, I think so…" I gulped air, as my heart pounded. The more air I took in the dizzier I felt. I must have teetered a bit because Molly reached out, caught me by the arm and steadied me.

"Come in and sit for a minute before you fall on your face."

"Thank you, Molly."

She walked me into the living room, and we sat on an antique sofa covered in deep green velvet and shiny braid. I looked around the room. Every piece of furniture was an antique, including the black dial phone, the large radio and the small black and white TV.

"Where's the dog?" she asked.

"He's sleeping at home. He does a lot of that. So Molly, how well do you know Lito?"

"Only met him once down by the mail box, but I've known the Oeblicks for about fifty years. The mother was a real piece a work. I'm not a gossip or anything, but I have to say she was a mean one. She and her husband worked those kids hard. They grew plants for the nursery in their back yard. Acres of them, and the kids did all the digging and potting."

"How long did that go on?" I asked.

"Until one-by-one they grew up and ran away. Jason's the only one who came back." Molly rubbed her double chin thoughtfully. "Jason was making pretty good money on the rodeo circuit. I heard that he and Daphne had a big house in Gilroy. And then they split up, Mr. Oeblick moved in and Jason moved in with his mother." Molly shook her head, unable to relate to such a family.

"Any idea who killed Mrs. Ocblick?" I asked.

"I'm no gossip, but I wouldn't put it past any of those kids. The way they were treated, I wouldn't blame them."

"Did you happen to see anyone over at the house the day she was murdered?"

"The Sheriff asked me that very question, and I told him I saw Caitlin and Lito, of course. And I saw a white van over there and one of those little Uber cars dropped someone off early in the morning. Kinda looked like Rico, but then I hadn't seen him in many years. Later I saw a black Mercedes parked in the driveway, and Jason's pickup was there and a few other cars. They were having a party."

"So who do you think did it?" I asked.

"Personally, I think it was Daphne. I don't like to gossip, but she's a real stinker. Wouldn't trust her as far as I could throw her, you know what I mean?"

"What about Mr. Oeblick?"

"Nah, what could he do? He's a lady killer with an overdue expiration date, in a wheelchair no less."

I nodded. "Nice talking with you, Molly." I stood up and walked to the door.

"Do you have to go?" she said.

"Yes, I have a hot date with my fiancé." I checked my watch and realized I had just one hour to trot home and bake the brownies I had promised to add to Alicia's home-cooked feast.

Chapter 19

Alicia signed her name on the dotted line, and so did Trigger when I told him that every runner would receive a really cool t-shirt for participating. I cornered Ernie in the kitchen, but he put up his hands and shook his head.

"I think I'm busy that day," he said, "but I'll give you a nice check instead."

Mom and Dad would be running, even though they would be turning eighty years old in one more year. I had their word over the phone. Knowing my mother, she would have a dozen friends signed up in no time. I just had to get the paperwork to her quickly so she would have time to get plenty of sponsors.

Two trips up Otis Road were more than my poor tired legs were used to, but homemade Mexican food and good conversation allowed me to forget my tired aching legs—mostly. I filled and emptied my plate one more time, but turned down dessert. When Alicia asked why, I told her I was dieting. She laughed and snorted until her sides hurt.

"Don't laugh, I love brownies and ice cream," I said, watching Alicia carry a tray of individual servings of vanilla ice cream topped with a brownie and drizzled with chocolate sauce to the table.

"Sorry, Jo, I know you're trying," Alicia said, and let out one last snort before she set the tray on the table.

I tried to stand up to help her serve the dessert, but my legs felt stiff and frozen. My back ached.

"Jo, what's the matter?" Ernie asked, as a concerned look washed over his face.

"I'm in training...."

We heard one stifled "snort" from Alicia, as she put a hand over her mouth and left the room to get spoons and cream for the coffee.

Trigger stood up, walked over to me and stood behind my chair. He put his hands on my upper back and gently massaged my upper back and neck. Not bad for a ten-year-old, I thought, closing my eyes and letting my body turn into mush. When Trigger stopped massaging my neck, I woke up with a start.

"Jo, would you like an icepack for your back?" Alicia asked.

"No, I'm fine, thanks. That was the best massage ever."

"How is the Oeblick case coming along?" she asked.

"I'm stuck. All four kids had plenty of hard feelings toward their mother, but no real motive to kill her. Two of them said they weren't at the house that day, but the neighbor across the street saw those two plus Fern. Everyone except Bea. She was probably under a bridge somewhere."

"Maybe the mailman did it," Ernie laughed. "Tell me again why Fern bought her mother's house."

"Because she had agreed to sell the Aromas house to her dad," I said, "so that he and Daphne can move into it. Jason owns half of the Gilroy house as part of the divorce settlement, so that's where he's going to live. It will be closer to the nursery, which he bought from his parents years ago. Basically, they're switching places."

"Personally, I'd rather live on Otis," Alicia said, as she cleared the table. "Your street is so pretty with all the oak trees and rolling hills."

"I wonder if my street will be the same with Daphne living there."

She laughed.

"Allie, I hate to eat and run, but we need to get over to Mom and Dad's before they go to bed." Still feeling tired and stiff, I looked forward to a hot bath at home. But not yet—duty called. I needed to get a sign-up sheet over to the folks. David had agreed to drive me to Santa Cruz. The Quintanas wished us luck, considering the winter road conditions.

David and I stepped outside into the frosty night, il-luminated by three-quarters of a moon and a billion stars. It was beautiful and romantic, but I would have rather had a balmy evening in the Bahamas. I shivered and zipped up my jacket. We climbed into the Miata icebox, put the heater on and waited for the heat to ar-rive. By the time we entered Highway One going north, we were warm and cozy.

"Look, David, all those cars pulled off the road. What's going on?"

He didn't answer. He was busy applying the brakes, skidding across two lanes and trying to miss a car parked against a bridge railing on our right. We nicked the SUV as we spun across a patch of black ice, coming to an unplanned stop against a delivery truck. Behind us, headlights zigged and zagged down the grade like roller skaters having a beer party.

"Get out of the car," David ordered.

"What? It's cold out there…." I whined.

"Out!" He opened my door and pulled me into the dark landscape, away from the car. "We'll be safer over here," David said, as we dashed over to a wire fence about twenty feet from the edge of the road. The drunk-en skaters were still coming, but the referees had joined the fun. Two Highway Patrol cars and a tow truck cre-ated a blinking light barrier at the edge of the ice.

Traffic came to a stop.

More patrol cars arrived.

David shared his insurance information with the driver of the SUV and the driver of the delivery truck. From there, we hopped into the Miata and waited for slow-moving patrol cars to lead traffic down the hill. David looked for an opening and eventually joined the parade.

By the time we arrived at Mom and Dad's, it was nine o'clock and all their lights were off. Immediately I worried that something was wrong with my parents.

"Looks like they went to bed. Did you tell them we were coming?" David asked.

"I forgot to call."

"We could push the paperwork under the door...."

"No, I want to see if everything is okay," I said, as my imagination jumped from illness to accident to old folks tied and gagged in a closet. As we stood on the front porch discussing what to do, the porch light flickered on.

The front door flew open and Dad stepped out wearing a 49ers t-shirt and boxer shorts.

"Dad, I was worried when I saw the lights were out."

"Your mother is sound asleep...."

"No I'm not," Mom said as she walked up next to Dad. She tied the belt on her robe and invited us in. I hadn't seen my mom in her "natural state" in many years. The years had been kind to her.

We sat down on the sofa.

Dad dropped into his chair and pulled a lap blanket over his bare legs.

I handed Mom the paperwork.

"I was so excited when you called and told me about the race. It sounds like a wonderful cause," she said. "I have fourteen people signed up to run and twenty-five signed up to be sponsors," Mom said. "Some of my friends think they're too old to run." She handed me forms full of information.

"Where did you get all this?" I asked.

"Downloaded it from the internet, of course."

"Okay…sorry we woke you up…."

"Don't worry about it, honey," Dad said. "We set out at five o'clock this morning on a hike up Mount Madonna. It was a group thing, and we ended up staying for dinner. Just got home an hour ago, but we cornered those hikers all right. They were as enthusiastic as we are, and most of them signed on the dotted line."

"When we got home we were so tired, we just went to bed," Mom said. "Oh, by the way, Myrtle left that for you." She pointed to a folded newspaper on the coffee table.

"Tell her thanks," I said, picking up the newspaper. "We should go and let you two get some rest."

David stood up and walked to the door. "Great to see you folks."

I stood beside him. Mom and Dad hugged each of us and stood at the door waving until the car pulled away. Halfway home, I was asleep dreaming sweet dreams of David and me traveling in a space craft up to Mount Madonna where we landed and met some earthlings having a winter solstice celebration. They stole our ship so we had to follow a scary path down the mountain in the dark.

Someone was tugging on my shoulder. I opened my eyes and there was David. We kissed and climbed out of the car. All was quiet and beautiful under the starry sky but cold enough to send us inside. Solow howled and sniffed us up and down, recognizing the scents of friends and family. We settled onto the sofa, and Solow snored at our feet.

After the Late Night News, David drove home and I went to bed. My eyes were open as my mind bounced from one silly idea to another. Across the room, Solow snored in his doggie bed while I tried to relax. But trying just made it worse. Ice cream was my usual remedy, so I got up, turned up the furnace and tried a bowl of mocha almond fudge with chocolate sauce on top.

When ice cream failed, I decided to read for a while. I was going to pick up a novel I hadn't finished reading yet, *All the Light We Cannot See.* It was good and I looked forward to finishing it, but the newspaper Myrtle gave me was lying on top of the book. I searched the paper for whatever she thought I should read.

Page four—there it was: *"Oeblick Case Stalled,"* and a photo of a man named Theodore Nottworth who looked very familiar. Who was he? I knew I'd seen him before. He was wanted for questioning.

I pored over the article, then read it again. According to the *Sentinel*, "Investigators think there may be a connection between Mrs. Oeblick's murder and a Silicon Valley chip smuggling ring." My first thought was, Doritos? But I quickly smacked that down in exchange for super secret computer chips. The article wanted to let the public know that the man in the picture may be headed for Mexico. Three people had been held by the police for questioning, and a member of the Oeblick family was also being questioned. Apparently chips were being stolen from a computer company, repackaged in Aromas and sent to China. The new technology was worth millions.

Instantly I thought of Fern. My jaw dropped as perspiration percolated across my forehead. I didn't like Fern, but I hated to see the Oeblick family in trouble. It sounded like Mrs. Oeblick had been in on the scheme as well. All of a sudden, the picture in the newspaper made sense. I had seen the man at the nursery. It was Ted, the delivery guy who had been looking for Fern. The guy who didn't like Mrs. Oeblick but liked her knitted goods, even though he was a polyester kind of guy, and not the type to wear hand-knitted accessories.

My mind went from second gear straight into over-drive. "There had to be a connection between knitted stuff and stolen chips," I said to Solow, who was curled at my feet. "It says here, the chips are half the size of a postage stamp." Was Mr. Oeblick involved or even aware of the scam? What about Jason and Bea? And Rico? I decided I would have to tread lightly around these people, since someone had already resorted to murder.

Chapter 20

After a fitful night's sleep, I pulled myself out of bed and began Monday morning with a wake-up shower and strong coffee. My plan for the day was to be as invisible as possible, quietly gathering information as I worked on the bucking horse mural. I loaded my painting gear into the back of the truck and hoisted Solow into the passenger seat. It was just another day of work at the nursery, except it wasn't. Nothing would be the same after that terrible newspaper article. I didn't know which Oeblick was the murderer. Fern looked pretty guilty, but I distrusted all of them.

The nursery greenery sparkled after an early morning sprinkle. The sun was out, Jason and his delivery truck were already gone, Bea and Caitlin were running things at the gift shop and Lito had already set out two ladders in front of the mural.

"Hey, Jo, I thought you'd never get here," Lito said, helping me unload the truck. "Jason wants it to look like this." He pulled a color photo out of his pocket to show me.

"Okay, white hat, camel-colored chaps and vest, blue shirt and pants and brown boots. I can do that. But first I have to paint the horse."

"What should I paint?" he asked.

"Can you paint clouds?"

"Sure, it's my specialty," he laughed.

"Okay, just a few along the ridge line. Don't overdo it."

Because the boy was tall, he didn't need to use a ladder. I took the little three-foot ladder since the slightly larger-than-life horse's head and shoulders would be about seven feet up from the bottom of the painting. The horse Jason wanted me to paint was a bucking quarter horse, brown with a white face. The photo showed a striped blanket under a typical brown western saddle.

I began sketching with a piece of white chalk and erasing with a damp cloth when necessary. Several times, I took time out to turn my back on the mural and point my little mirror at the picture, giving me a "fresh" look at the drawing over my shoulder. The final look in the mirror was interrupted when a blue delivery truck pulled into the parking lot. The door slammed as the engine labored. Exhaust spewed from the tailpipe. The driver ran into the gift shop. Whatever he wanted, his disgruntled expression said he didn't get it. He hopped back into his truck, spewed gravel and turned right onto Highway 152, better known as Hecker Pass.

Finally satisfied with the drawing, I mixed three batches of brown paint. The first was the basic deep chestnut brown of the horse, the second was a lighter brown and the third was even lighter. Horses are wonderful examples of the beauty of muscle, contour and shiny coat. For me the toughest part of painting them was doing justice to their strength and character.

Thinking about character, suddenly my thoughts went back to the stinky tailpipe and ugly man-bun driver.

"Oh my God!" I said to Lito. "That was Ted, the guy they're looking for."

"Huh? What are you talking about?"

"Never mind," I said as I ran to my truck. "Just clean up when you're done."

Solow followed me, sensing something was up. He howled just before I tossed him into his seat. A minute later, we were on Hecker Pass Road heading west. I fumbled around in my purse for my cell phone, as we swayed side to side in our seats, taking the hairpin turns like a race car driver. I hadn't charged my phone in the last few days, and sure enough it was dead. I wanted to call 911, but phone booths didn't exist any more now that everyone carried their own personal cell phones.

Ted was about ten minutes ahead of me, but the way I was driving I knew I could catch up to him. If he was going to Aromas, I would discretely follow him.

"Oh, darn it!"

Solow put his head down.

"Not you, my sweet puppy, I'm upset with the slow-poke idiot driver in front of us. Some people shouldn't be driving."

Bright sunlight gave way to shade as we motored up through a heavily wooded area. I blinked and stared ahead as my eyes adjusted. The little car in front of us kept to the speed limit and so did I since there was a double yellow line and no passing allowed on the two-lane, curvy road. But a highway patrol car parked at the side of the road had me singing a different tune, thanking the little car ahead for keeping me at the proper speed.

My infatuation with the car ahead didn't last long. If only I could get past the little snot. But I couldn't. I blinked my headlights and told Solow how frustrated I was. Did the driver have to brake at every turn, while descending the mountain? I understood that people who were new to the road were usually scared spit-less, but that was no excuse.

Finally we hit bottom and increased our speed on the half-mile of straight flat highway.

We came to a four-way stop.

"Don't turn left!" I shouted at the windshield.

He turned left.

I sped up behind the little compact slug and passed him easily. Now to find the blue delivery truck. We entered Highway 129, a flat, curvy two-lane road. Noontime traffic moved along at the speed limit. I couldn't pass the cluster of a dozen or more cars ahead of me, so I drove responsibly, biting my nails down to nubs.

Solow took the last half of the trip in his stride, passed out, paws twitching.

We rolled through Aromas. Three cars ahead, I spotted a blue delivery truck chugging up the hill. Deciding to be discreet, I kept my speed down and followed at a distance. He turned onto Otis. Now I was ninety-nine percent sure he was headed for Jason's house—soon to be Fern's and then Mr. Oeblick's. We passed David's house, then mine. A few more turns and a dozen mailboxes later, we had Jason's house and the blue truck on the left and Molly Pearson's house on the right.

Suddenly I lost my nerve and swerved into Molly's driveway. A metal fence cut across the concrete halfway to the house. Should I get out and jump the fence or just turn around and go home where we would be safe? As I thought about my choices, the long gate in front of me began sliding to one side. My new friend led a lonely life and was obviously inviting me in for a visit.

I parked the truck, sprinted (ouch) to the front door and breathlessly asked Molly if I could use her phone. She pointed to the old black telephone in the hall. As I dialed 911, her eyes opened wide and her fleshy cheeks reddened with excitement. All the way to Aromas, I had practiced what I would say to the operator, but practice doesn't help much when excitement and fear rise to a certain level.

"He's wanted for questioning in the Oeblick case and the chip case...."

"Chip case?"

"Yeah, super secret chips being sent to China."

"Ma'am, do you feel you are in danger?"

"Of course not, I'm at my friend's house across the street...."

"A sheriff will be there within the hour."

"We need help now. Who knows how long Ted will be here," I said, as I stared at Jason's house from Molly's front window.

Ted and Jason came out of the house and stood talking in the driveway.

"Josephine, he's getting in the truck. What should we do?" Molly panted.

"Thanks for the phone. I need to go...."

Molly followed me out to the truck faster than a toupee in a hurricane, and climbed in.

Solow saw her coming and crawled off the seat just in time. The only place left for him was on top of her Birkenstocks.

Molly pounded on the dash, "He's getting away!"

"Don't worry, that big old truck doesn't go very fast. And he's probably being careful not to get pulled over for speeding," I said, as we followed him down the road to my house.

"What in the world!" I slammed on the brakes, put the truck in reverse and parked at the side of the road. "What is he doing in my house?"

Molly's jaw dropped, as we peered through the wild lilacs growing along the front of my property. "He walked right in! Don't you lock your doors?" She turned to look at me like an incredulous mother would look at her wayward child.

"I lock the doors when I take Solow with me. But sometimes I forget."

Molly rolled her eyes.

"Did you lock up your house when we left?" I asked.

"No, there wasn't time...."

"What is he doing in there?" I said, wondering if two unarmed women and a very short dog could tackle a younger, stronger, possibly armed man. Minutes ticked by. Thinking about it wasn't getting the job done. We discussed every attack plan, especially the one where we arm ourselves with shovels and hoes, but the logistics weren't good. The tool shed was behind the house, and we would probably be seen trying to get there.

"Good morning, ladies," Ted said, his face in my window.

Solow let out several sharp barks. Even he hadn't seen the slick man until that moment.

Ted invited us into his truck, and yanked my door open before I had time to lock it (the story of my life).

Molly scrambled out of her seat, ready to escape.

"You!" he pointed to the sixty-year-old out-of-shape woman. "Get in my truck or I'll hurt your friend."

"What's this all about?" I asked, indignantly.

"That's what I'd like to know. You're the ones following me—remember?" He grabbed my arm and pulled me out of my seat. On my way out the door, I tried to grab my purse, but he knocked it away with his big hairy hand.

Molly trudged up the gravel driveway like the convicted to the gallows, to the back of the delivery truck.

Solow walked behind us. When he tried to follow us into the back of the truck, Ted kicked him away.

Solow cried and ran to the porch.

Tears came to my eyes when I thought about my poor dog, kicked and left to fend for himself. But I knew he would head over to David's house as soon as it was dinnertime. The real question was what would happen to us—two helpless women going who knows where. And why was this man in my house in the first place?

The doors slammed, the engine fired up and the truck beeped as it backed down my driveway and onto Otis Road. We swayed with the turns, having nothing to hold onto except one potted miniature palm tree that slid around more than both of us put together.

"Molly, do you have a phone in your pocket?"

"Of course not. My phone is black with a ten-foot cord, remember?"

In the dim light, I felt free to roll my eyes. Who in the world didn't have a cell phone? Of all the people in the universe—and I'm locked in the back of a truck with Molly.

Feeling sorry for myself, my thoughts included how cold the back of a truck could be. I shivered and wished I had grabbed my knitted hat and scarf from behind the driver's seat. But if I had had time to grab the knitted stuff, it would have been second to grabbing my purse.

Our ride in the delivery truck would have been funny, if we weren't being kidnapped. I looked at Molly as our butts bumped along the floor to the right, and the next turn jerked and rolled us all the way back to where we started. We tried holding hands to see if that would keep us from bumping and sliding. Her hand was hot and wet, mine freezing. If we had been two guys, we would probably be the perfect temperature one-hundred-percent of the time, and we would have already invented some gadget to keep us from sliding across the floor using metal junk we found in our Levi pockets.

"Where do you think we're going?" Molly asked.

"I don't know, but offhand I'd say we're going to hell in a hand basket. Actually, I've met this guy before. His name is Ted, and even at the time I thought something wasn't right about him and his stupid man-bun."

"His driving is terrible," Molly said, as my hand left hers because my body was being thrown across the floor and slammed into the opposite metal wall. Two-seconds later, Molly rolled across the floor and smashed into me.

"I'm so sorry...."

"Don't worry about it, Molly, just think of a way out of here."

"Yes, I'll work on that," she mumbled. "Did you say you're raising money for the homeless in Gilroy?"

"Yeah, people sign up to run and other people promise so much money for each mile their runner runs. So far I have a check from you, but no actual sponsors. Why do you ask?"

"Oh, I'm talking just to keep from crying," she said. "Does it feel like we're on the freeway?"

"Now that you mention it, yeah. No more sharp turns, thank goodness. I think we're traveling pretty fast, but I have no clue if we're going north or south. Wonder if he's taking us to Mexico?"

"Oh, Josephine, I don't think...you think he would?" her voice trembled.

"No, don't worry, we'll find a way out of here." But I didn't believe a word of what I just said. I pinched the light button on my watch and figured we had been traveling for at least half an hour, or approximately thirty-something miles. If we were going south, we would be arriving in Salinas or Monterey soon. If we were going north, we should be in Morgan Hill by now.

"Oh, that was a quick stop," Molly said. "Now we're turning left...I think we're going through a town with all these stops."

"You're right, and they aren't stop signs. They're stop lights because we have to wait so long. Oh, we're going up a steep hill," I said, as we slid against the back doors. "That cancels the southern flat lands. We must be going north."

Molly agreed with my evaluation.

Molly and I were suddenly pressed against the back doors as the truck roared up a hill, which I had already guessed was Hill Street and made a sharp right turn into Fern's driveway. We heard the garage door open, the truck moved forward and the garage door closed with a thud. The truck door slammed and then all was quiet, except for the purr of the motor in neutral.

"He didn't turn the motor off!" Molly cried.

"Yeah, just when everything was going so well," I quipped.

"I'm feeling sick," she said. "We have to get out of...did you hear that?"

"Yeah, it's the garage door opening...." I said, listening carefully. The door stayed open, a car door slammed, a house door slammed and shortly after that we heard angry voices coming from inside the house. We couldn't make out the words, but a female voice went ballistic on a male voice. More doors slammed and the truck engine went dead, just about the time I was feeling drowsy and sick to my stomach from the carbon monoxide spewing from the tailpipe.

It was too early for high-fives, but we had been given a reprieve.

The voices came closer. We heard every word of Fern's conversation with Ted.

"Don't you ever try something like that again," she said. "I just hope it's not too late. Unlock these doors now!"

We heard the garage door close as Ted spewed ugly words. He opened the back doors of the truck and peeked in. Somehow Molly and I had the same idea at the same time. We lay on the floor, eyes closed, still as cats watching their prey.

A hand reached in and touched my ankle.

"They're alive," Ted hissed.

"We'll deal with them in a minute," Fern said. "Did you get anything out of Jason?"

"He still says he doesn't have it. He's a good liar if you ask me."

"You're right about the lying, but remember he's my brother...."

"Brother, schmother, he's a liar," Ted growled.

Chapter 21

After a rough ride in the back of Ted's truck and exhaust poisoning on top of that, I was madder than a pack of she-wolves. But all I had with me was an older, slower woman named Molly.

A door slammed and all was quiet.

Molly raised her head off the cold metal floor of Ted's delivery truck.

I put a finger in front of my mouth and shook my head for her to be quiet. We waited a few more seconds to make sure Fern and Ted had left the garage.

"I'm going to push the button," I whispered, pointing to the door to the house. "Get ready to go under the garage door as it goes up. Here I go!"

I leaped off the back of the truck and sprinted to the opposite side of the garage, pushed the button positioned next to the door to the laundry room and ran back to Molly as she carefully climbed out of the truck. The garage door was halfway up as we ducked down and under it. I pulled her through the opening and on up the driveway. To say that Molly was not athletic or even flexible would be an understatement. She moved like an out-of-shape, heavy-set, sixty-year-old, which she was.

"Come on, Molly, you can do this. He tried to murder us," I said, breathlessly. "You know he's not going to let us go...down!" I pulled her to the ground behind a neighbor's rosemary bush. She flattened out like a rug on a rock.

"Ouch," she whispered.

"Shhh!"

"Josephine, I'm going to sneeze...."

"Don't!"

"But I'm allergic to rosemary...."

"Pretend its hibiscus," I snapped. "Sorry, just don't sneeze. Okay, he went back in the house, probably to tell Fern we got away. Let's run up Hill Street to the next door house before they get back." I pointed to the Tudor-style two-story house on the right.

"Up there?" Why not go down the hill...?"

"Because that's what they'll expect us to do." I pulled Molly up, and we loped, at Molly-speed, across a hundred feet of soggy lawn. At the far end of the grass, we turned right and headed down fifty feet of cobbled driveway connecting us with a three-car garage. At the corner of the building, a concrete path led to the back-yard gate. Garbage cans, a blue plastic tarp and a bucket full of gardening tools blocked our way.

Molly panted, holding her ribs, as I rolled the garbage cans away from the six-foot-gate and emptied the bucket. I turned the bucket upside down, pushed it up against the redwood gate and stepped up onto it. My nose hit the top of the fence as I scanned the back yard for dogs and other hazards. Trying not to worry about redwood slivers, I pulled myself up, right leg first. With arms and one leg up, I hung there for a moment gathering my strength.

"Are you all right, Josephine?" Molly whispered, as she stepped closer and pushed on my ribs with both hands.

"Just catching my breath," I said. After a couple gulps of air, I hoisted my right leg and hip over the top, twisted and dropped down onto a skateboard someone had left behind. I wanted to say, "Ouch," but didn't dare.

The beep, beep, beep of a truck backing up got my attention and prickled my skin. Quickly, I stood up and unlocked the gate.

"Molly, where are you?" I whispered.

"Right here," she said, as she crawled out from under the blue tarp and hurried through the open gate. "The truck backed up, so I hid."

"Nice work, Molly. Let's go sit in that gazebo over there by the pool. Maybe Ted will stop looking for us in an hour or two."

Molly shivered. "I guess a little enclosure is better than none."

My windbreaker was next to useless, and poor Molly hadn't had time to grab a jacket when we left her house. We stretched out on two of the five short benches circling the open-air gazebo.

"Molly, do you see what I see?"

She sat up and looked around. "Like what?"

"I think I saw someone in that window." I pointed to a kitchen window overlooking the back yard, the pool and the Santa Clara Valley beyond. From Hill Street, all the houses looked like they were two stories because they were built on the side of a steep hill. The garages were built into the ground in the front constituting a third floor when viewed from the back, with the kitchen and living room as the second floor and bedrooms on the third floor.

"Do you think these people will call the police?" Molly asked.

"I certainly hope so. That's who we need right now." I stood up and walked over to a back door and knocked.

Footsteps stopped at the door. "Who's there?" a woman's voice shouted.

"Josephine and Molly. We need to call the police...."

"Why?" she shouted back.

"We were kidnapped by someone running from the police!" I yelled.

The door cracked open a couple inches. A chain kept it there.

"Show me some ID," the woman demanded.

"We don't have any. He snatched us and we had no time to get our purses. Please, just call 911 and let me tell them what happened," I begged.

Molly walked up behind me and peered at the lady through the crack in the door. "We're nice people, really we are," she said sweetly.

The woman pulled her phone out of a pocket and punched in 911. She handed the phone to me through the space under the chain.

"911 emergency..." The operator asked me all the usual questions and I answered the best I could. No, we weren't in danger at present. No, we didn't know where Ted was headed. No, we had not been harmed, except for some dizziness and nausea from carbon monoxide asphyxiation.

The operator told me that the police response time was forty-five minutes to an hour.

"But tell the police that Ted and Fern are the ones involved in the Silicon Valley chip scandal. They're somewhere in Morgan Hill or Gilroy right now. Don't let them get away. They tried to kill us."

The chain clattered to the wall and the door opened.

"I'm sorry, ladies, I had to be sure you were harmless—I mean nice people, you know what I mean. I have kids...."

"We understand, ma'am," Molly said, shivering in the cold.

The woman said everyone called her "Fluff" and invited us into her garage. Maybe she felt sorry for us with our blue lips and trembling bodies. Two-thirds of the three-car garage was packed solid with large plastic storage containers stacked eight feet high. An extra large SUV was parked against the far wall.

"What's all this?" I blurted, like it was any of my business.

"Oh, holiday stuff. You know, decorations and stuff, that's why they call me Fluff," she giggled. "Would you like to come upstairs and have some hot cocoa?"

"Yes, thank you, that would be just wonderful," Molly said, as she and I followed Fluff up a flight of stairs to a large kitchen like no other. Our jaws dropped as we looked around. There were pilgrim salt shakers and place mats on the table, little Indian wigwams decorated the long granite counter tops and pictures of turkeys were everywhere. The pattern on the tablecloth was autumn leaves.

"Looks like Thanksgiving around here," I said, staring at a five-foot tall quilted and stuffed turkey surrounded by plastic pumpkins with smiley faces.

"Yes, and I just finished decorating upstairs." After a tour of the house, we sipped our hot drinks at the kitchen table amongst pilgrims, Indians and turkeys. Fluff wanted to know details about our capture and escape. Her brown eyes grew big as I explained much of what had happened, and Molly added to it. The tour and hot cocoa lasted forty-five minutes, and then the doorbell rang.

Fluff hurried to the door and let the policeman in. She offered him hot cocoa and a seat at the table, but he said he needed to see about another call as soon as possible. The four of us moved into the living room and sat on the edge of sofas full of holiday pillows.

By this time, Molly was excited and began telling the story with enthusiasm. I added information here and there. Since we had no blood or open wounds, it was sounding like it might become a tale of "they said—we said."

The policeman looked slightly bored. He checked his phone, said he would be looking for the blue delivery truck and excused himself to go to another call. Apparently someone had run through a red light.

I rolled my eyes and wished him luck, under my breath, as he climbed into his cruiser. He backed up and roared down the hill, not even looking at the house next door.

"Fluff, would you mind if I borrow your phone one more time? I need to call my fiancé to get a ride home."

"Not at all. I would drive you myself, but I need to pick up the kids from school in a few minutes. I'll drop you at the coffee shop, and he can pick you up there." Fluff pulled a jacket out of the coat closet and put it on, demonstrating her need to leave.

"Thank you Stuff, I mean Fluff. I hope we won't make you late...." I said, as the three of us took the stairs down to the garage and piled into the SUV. Thankfully, the vehicle had only a few decorations in it like the autumn leaf patterned seat covers and pilgrim stencils on the side windows.

At the bottom of the hill, we left Hill Street and cruised east on Cochran. Fluff stopped the car and let us out at the local coffee shop, the one I told David about. Over the phone, he didn't ask too many questions, mainly he wanted to know if we were okay. Sitting at the counter, gazing at trays full of donuts, I was feeling much better. When I asked the barista for two glasses of water, he looked down his freckled nose at me. "Beware of kids with titles," I thought to myself.

But the water arrived, and after a while, so did David.

"Josie, how did you lose your truck?" He cocked his head to one side, as a quirky smile crossed his lips. I hadn't told him the whole story over the phone.

"I didn't lose it. It's at home. David, this is our neighbor and my new friend, Molly."

"Let me guess, you live across the street from the Oeblicks?" David laughed.

Molly smiled. "How did you know that?"

"Psychic, I guess. Actually, Josephine said you live at the end of the road."

I turned to Molly. "I'm trying to solve the Oeblick murder mystery. He hates it when I get involved in these things."

She looked up at the ceiling. "I get it now. Josephine, maybe you're getting close to solving the murder and that's why we were kidnapped."

"You didn't say anything about being kidnapped," David said, as his smart aleck smile disappeared. "Who kidnapped you?"

"Ted had us in his delivery truck, and he left the engine running with the garage door closed," I said.

"Are you girls okay?" David asked, his forehead showing major worry lines.

Molly and I looked at each other. "We're okay, aren't we, Josephine?"

"Yeah, we'll be all right," I said under my breath, not feeling sure about anything.

"So where is your truck?"

"I told you, it's at home with Solow and my purse," I sighed.

"So you used Molly's phone to call me...?"

"No, we used Fluff's phone, since we had already climbed the fence. She was very nice. She even dropped us off here at the coffee shop."

David shook his head. "What's a Fluff?"

"Fluff is a nickname. She's a very nice lady. It's a long story—can we have a donut while we talk about it?"

David finally realized we didn't have our purses, money, phones, etc., and we were way-past-lunch hungry. Consequently, my gallant boyfriend treated us to coffee and donuts at three in the afternoon. We told him more than he really wanted to know.

Molly obviously had goo-goo eyes for David. I didn't mind. She could look, but not touch. I asked her if she had always lived alone in her big house on Otis. She said her husband had died of a heart attack at age fifty-two. She had raised her son in that house and planned to stay there.

"So the police said they were looking for this Ted character?" David asked.

I thought the discussion was over, but David had so many questions. I swallowed a bite of donut and washed it down with a sip of coffee.

"A policeman came to the house, and we told him everything that had happened. He wrote it all down, and told us he would look into it. Then he left."

"The nice policeman looked very concerned when we told him how Ted had closed the garage door and left us in the truck with the engine running," Molly added. A female customer at the next table stared at her in disbelief.

"And all Fern wanted to know was if Ted had gotten something from Jason, whatever that means." Suddenly it occurred to me that the one thing Ted and Fern had in common was they both loved Mrs. Oeblick's knitted items. I thought about my hat and scarf. They were nice looking, for knits, but there was nothing artistic or extraordinary about them. My thoughts went to my truck, unlocked, parked behind a wild lilac bush near my home. My purse and the hat and scarf were easy pickins if someone noticed the truck wasn't locked.

I stood up. "Guess we should be going."

David stood up and paid the tab at the counter.

Molly wrapped the last two donuts in a napkin and reluctantly followed us out the door. Tucked away at the end of Otis, I wondered if she had a social life of any kind. On the way home, I asked her what her hobbies were.

"I like to write." She swallowed a bite of powdered sugar donut. "I write articles for local newspapers, websites and such." White sugar floated everywhere, from her chins down to the leather seats.

"I wonder if Sugarbell and the homeless people could use some advertising for the projects they're trying to get started," I said, twisting around in the front seat to face her in the back.

"Actually, it's my profession," she said, "but I wouldn't mind doing some pro-bono work for a good cause."

"And we could make posters to advertise the race," I said.

Molly seemed to like that idea too. "My work room is equipped to handle that. I have a large stock of paper and a color printer that will handle up to fourteen by eighteen inch sheets. Glossy or flat paper."

"What are you doing this evening?" I asked.

David gave me "a look." Like, what do you think you're doing?

"Nothing special, I guess," she said.

"Perfect! It's almost five. We'll have an early dinner, and I'll drop by your place about seven?"

"Ah, sure," she said.

David parked the Miata in Molly's driveway and spoke to her as she climbed out of the backseat. "Are you sure you aren't traumatized after the kidnapping today?"

"I'll be okay, but it will be nice to have Josephine with me this evening. I don't want to be alone."

I didn't want to be alone either, and I would have preferred David's company, but I sensed that Molly was still feeling a bit shaken. I should know, since that was how I felt. Besides, I planned to spy on Jason's house. She had the perfect view of the place.

Chapter 22

My plan was to paint a bucking horse Tuesday, but I decided there was no reason to hurry. After Monday's horrendous kidnapping, I planned to take my time with the mural painting, collect my thoughts and stay safe. David had lectured me on the safety subject every which way he could, pointing out how lucky I was that Molly and I weren't injured and nothing had been stolen from my truck. But I did have a mess to clean up. Ted had emptied the bookshelves and tossed everything in my closet onto the floor. He even scrounged around in the loft, leaving quite a mess.

Monday night, after David and I had put all my belongings away, he took Solow for a short walk and then went home. I had had quite a day, but I wasn't ready to quit yet. I drove up to Molly's place with all the information I had on the homeless project, including a couple of newspaper articles. She wrote a nice article about the race, added pictures and submitted it to several local papers. With only five days till Saturday, we hoped the papers would print it on short notice.

Taking charge of the poster department, I found pictures on the internet of Holiday Park and its inhabitants. I created a digital collage from the pictures and Molly added the verbiage, including all pertinent information. She printed thirty-five posters on glossy fourteen by eighteen sheets of paper.

While Molly printed posters, I borrowed her binoculars and took a break on the front porch. The stars were out and the porch light was off. It was cold and I was about to go back inside when I heard voices from across the street. Several cars were parked in Jason's driveway, but it was too dark to tell colors and models. Light shone from almost every window. Was Jason having a party?

As I moseyed quietly across the street, a chilly breeze smacked my face. I stopped at the edge of the road and leaned against the trunk of an old oak tree, listening to a conversation between a man and a woman silhouetted in front of a picture window. The man was nicely built, whereas the woman was tall and skinny. Most likely it was Rico and Olive—I mean Fern.

"Don't lecture me, sis. You're in more trouble than I ever thought of getting into. You must be out of your mind...." He laughed a wicked laugh.

"What do you know, little brother? You've been gone so long. You never had to put up with our dysfunctional family, our nasty mother, lying brother and a homeless sister who doesn't know up from down."

"Bea's not so bad, just too much bad luck. You should take it easy on her."

"You think she'd do the same for me?" Fern snarked. "She'd probably volunteer to be a hostile witness at my trial."

"Good will has to start somewhere. Actually, I don't really care. I'm getting outta here soon as I can raise some travel money."

"I suppose you're going to ask me...."

"Not even for the time of day," he said, turning and walking into Jason's house.

A car door slammed, rubber peeled and a black sedan sped down the road.

I crossed the street and entered Molly's house, where I found her in her workroom finishing up a slice of pumpkin pie swimming in half-melted vanilla ice cream. She looked up. Her cheeks were red.

"Would you like a piece of pie, Josephine?"

"Sure, I need some comfort food right now."

Molly nodded like she knew what I was talking about.

"I accidentally overheard a conversation...."

"Yes, sound carries very well around here, doesn't it? Country evenings are so quiet...except for the people across the street."

"So you've heard things from Jason's house?" I asked, following her into the kitchen.

Molly cut a piece of pie for me and plopped a scoop of ice cream on top.

"I think I heard a scream the night Mrs. Oeblick fell off the balcony, around ten o'clock. The nightly news had just come on."

"Really? You heard a scream? What kind of balcony?" I asked.

"I've seen the fancy iron railing on her balcony. Her bedroom is on the second floor in the back of the house." Molly scraped her plate with her spoon, put the last bite in her mouth and closed her eyes for a couple seconds.

"Sounds like she landed on her head," I said, remembering the newspaper mentioning a knot on the top of her head and a broken neck.

Molly nodded. "I'm awfully tired...."

"Sorry, Molly, I shouldn't have stayed so long. I'm exhausted too."

But I didn't sleep well that night, between ugly nightmares about people falling on their heads and wakeful hours of listening to a spooky sounding windstorm whistling around the outside of my house. Something slapped and banged against my window.

A coyote howled.

I wondered if the windows and doors were locked.

Maybe a cookie and hot chocolate would help me to fall asleep. I slipped on my robe and checked the kitchen door and the front door to make sure they were locked. Solow followed me and my bag of cookies back to the living room where I stretched out on the sofa, sipped cocoa and hoped the TV would lull me to sleep.

One thought kept bouncing around in my head as I watched a very old rerun on TV. What was Ted looking for? What if he was looking for my turquoise hat and scarf? After all, they originally came from the same batch of knits that Fern had been so determined to have.

"Wap, bang, thud."

As awful as the weather outside sounded, I knew I would have to venture out. Something was loose and flapping against the house, and I needed to know what it was.

Solow ignored my call to duty, pretending he was asleep.

I grabbed a flashlight and stuffed it into the pocket of a coat I wore over my robe. When I opened the front door, a wet wind came at me slanting in from the west. The wind chimes dangling from the porch roof were loud and tangled. Their song was chaos.

Since I was already outside, I decided to get my hat and scarf out of the truck and put them to good use. They warmed me for a minute or two, and then they were wet. I ignored my discomfort and pointed the flashlight at the path leading to the back yard. My flimsy fluffy slippers squished along, becoming more and more useless.

The thuds became louder as I approached the far corner of the house. The light stream glommed onto a little black box at the end of three feet of wire hanging from the eaves directly over my bedroom window. It wasn't something I could reach, let alone fix, so I finished circling the house and hurried inside. I figured once I knew the problem was a little black box, I would be able to sleep.

All nestled in my warm bed, listening to the rhythm of the dangling box hitting the wall, I finally relaxed and let sleep find me.

A short time later, still in a half-asleep fog, I sat up in bed. The thuds had stopped, and it occurred to me that I had never seen the little box before. What was it and why was it there?

I checked the clock. It was ten after five, might as well get up.

That's how my Tuesday at the nursery started. Bea said I looked like something three cats had dragged in, each one doing damage. Jason offered me a second cup of coffee, and Caitlin told me to man the shop while she shoveled trenches to contain last night's rainwater drainage problems. I yawned and watched her work from my seat by the heater.

The sun came out around noon, and by twelve-thirty I was drawing a bucking horse all over again. The rainstorm had washed away the chalk from my first efforts. Drawing the horse was easier this time since it was a second try. My plan was to fill in the horse using the dark chestnut brown and create the muscles, shadows and highlights the next day—after a good night's sleep.

Lito thumbed his way over to the nursery. He arrived around ten and leaned against my truck watching me paint.

I asked him a silly question, "Do you know much about electronics?"

Lito laughed. "I'm seventeen, it's in my DNA."

"Last night I found a small black box, maybe metal—maybe plastic, dangling on a wire from the rafters outside my bedroom window. Do you know what it could be?"

"Lots of things. Probably something old, like for the phone or cable or something like that."

"I never saw it until last night. But, yeah, it could have been up in the eaves and I never noticed it."

The horse was already half painted. It would be a short paint day.

"Do you have time to ride with me to my house and take a look?"

"Sure, I'm between projects," Lito laughed.

"What projects?"

"That's just it—I don't have any."

"You're such a good artist, Lito, I'd love to see you working on a mural."

"I've asked around, but who trusts a seventeen-year-old to do a good job?"

"You're right. Finish painting this horse and then we'll go to my house."

Lito looked a little worried.

"Just paint it solid brown and I'll add shadows, highlights and white markings tomorrow. Maybe I'll have time to paint the blanket and saddle too." I handed him the brush I was using and walked over to the shop to get my purse. I asked Caitlin if it would be all right for Lito to help me with the painting and later with a project at my house.

"Just so he's home by six-thirty. His dad gets upset if Lito isn't home when he gets home from work."

I poured myself a cup of lukewarm coffee, gulped it down and left the nursery as Jason was arriving from delivering trees to San Jose and Cupertino. He waved as our vehicles rolled by each other. Once I joined the Hecker Pass traffic, I turned on the radio and rolled my window down. A nap would have been beneficial, but I had other ideas and not enough time.

Reaching the outskirts of Gilroy, I pulled my truck off the road and called David. I told him not to bake anything in my oven.

"What are you talking about, Josie? I hardly ever use your oven...."

"Well, don't use it today. I have something in it."

"See you tonight?" he asked.

"I think so." My mind was mostly on the package I was hiding. If someone turned my oven on, the knitted hat and scarf wrapped in newspaper would catch fire like dry twigs in a firebox. I made a mental note to take the package out of the oven when I got home, and hide it somewhere else. But where?

"Josie, honey, are you there?"

"Oh, sorry David, see you tonight." We hung up.

I pulled back into traffic heading into town. It was noon, I was hungry and I happened to be nearing the hot dog place. Sugarbell greeted me at the take out window. I paid for my four chili dogs and two sodas and parked at the outer edge of the parking lot. Minutes later, Sugarbell climbed into the passenger seat.

"Would you like a chili dog?" I asked.

"Are you kidding? That's all I eat around here. But don't get me wrong—I appreciate the offer. I've been dying to talk to you, Josephine. Mom doesn't tell me much, but I read the papers. Looks like Fern may be going to jail. What do you think?"

"I think you're right, but I'm wondering if some of the evidence is missing."

"Like, what evidence?" she asked.

"Maybe the cops don't know how the chips were being smuggled out of the country...."

"What gave you that idea?"

"Oh, just thinking." I took another bite of hot dog.

"Things are really heating up around here," Sugarbell said. "We have over a thousand people signed up for the run, and my boss said that after the race all their hot dog profits will go to the homeless. Well, Mac-Ducks got wind of that and they're going to do the same thing. Now Burger Buns is thinking about it. Can you add that to your posters?"

"We can make new posters with that information included, but try to get Burger Buns pinned down right away. We'll have to hurry on it, only four days left," I said, feeling like creating new posters was the least Molly and I could do. "My mom signed up a lot of runners and sponsors and I have some checks for you." I dug around in my purse and located the checks I had collected from my neighbors.

Sugarbell thumbed through the checks. "Five-hundred dollars!" She held up the check from Molly. "Nice work, Josephine. Did you see the article in the paper today about the people in the Holiday Camp?"

"No, what about it?"

"Besides the pictures, they talked about our efforts to keep the park clean; and they had positive things to say about our veterans, and they were very sympathetic to our little families. They talked about the race and several events that will be happening afterward, like a five-dollar-a-plate spaghetti dinner at the grange. All the food is donated and all profits go to our projects, like haircuts and clothing for people who want to interview for jobs."

With all of Sugarbell's good news dancing through my head, I barely remembered to stop at the nursery to pick up Lito. He had already finished painting the horse, and had washed the brushes and stowed the gear. He ate chili dogs while I drove us over the mountain. We ended up in Aromas around two o'clock.

Solow was so happy to see us. He followed Lito, who followed me down the path and around the house to the far back window. I pointed to the box.

Because Lito was much taller than I, and it was full daylight, he had a better look at the dangling thing. It turned out to be a plastic box of a type he said he recognized. But to be sure, he pulled out his phone and Googled the information he wanted.

"I hate to tell you this, Josephine, but that's a listening device that also sends out pictures and video. Someone can control it from miles away."

I suddenly felt heat in my cheeks. "A peeping Tom?"

"I guess you could say that, but more than one person can watch the video," he said, glancing at his shoes.

"Could they put it on YouTube?"

He shrugged. "Guess they could."

My heart pounded like a throttled motorboat. I pictured myself in a movie where I was the one and only star, climbing out of bed looking like Dracula's mother-in-law. Who would have the nerve to do this?

Suddenly I was furious.

I kicked the wall. "Ouch!"

"Take it easy, Josephine. I'll disconnect this thing and hopefully it hasn't been here very long. It's a new model—came out a couple of months ago."

"So it could have been up there for two months?" My voice squeaked.

"Minus shipping time...."

"Actually it was probably there no more than a week or two," I said. "Ted tossed my house a couple days ago, so I know he knows where I live. He's been looking for...."

"Josephine, don't say any more until I get this thing disconnected."

I slapped my hands over my mouth and tried to recall what I had just belted out.

"I'll need a ladder," Lito said.

I pointed down the path to my tin shed. Silently I told myself not to say another word until the box was destroyed.

"Oh, and Lito, bring a hammer with you."

Chapter 23

Thinking back to Tuesday, I was fit to be fried. Even though I had smashed the vermin black box with a hammer until it looked like it had gone through a shredder fifty times, anger had me by the throat. Trying to think positively, I told myself that Wednesday was a new day and things would be better. But in my experience, it's pretty hard to fool one's self.

It was the day before Thanksgiving, and David had decided to have the big turkey meal at his house. Mom, Dad and Myrtle were invited plus David's son Harley and five-year-old granddaughter Monica. When I asked if Molly, Lito and Caitlin could be invited, he said that would be fine.

I decided I wouldn't finish painting the bucking horse until Friday. Instead, I would make new posters with Molly, and help David prepare the Thanksgiving feast. Cooking was never my "thing," but I offered to run errands for him.

The phone rang early Wednesday morning.

"Hi, Molly, I'm glad you called. Would you like to join us for turkey day at David's house?"

"That would be lovely. Thank you, Josephine."

"Oh, and we need to make new posters...."

"You're kidding!"

"No I'm not kidding. I have new information about some great moneymakers. We should send out another article for the papers too, now that the hot dog place, MacDucks and Burger Bun are all going to donate their profits. And the spaghetti dinner should bring in a bunch of money too."

"That's wonderful, Josephine."

"Is ten o'clock good?"

"Sure, come on up here whenever you're ready," Molly said.

"We'll have breakfast and then run up there," I said, visualizing Solow and I running up the road, practicing for the race. I visualized myself being bumped around and stomped on by thousands of sweaty people running through downtown Gilroy. Not a pretty picture, so I erased it from my mind.

Solow and I arrived at Molly's place a little before nine, winded and sweating even though it was a very cool day. Each of us knew just what to do since we had produced articles and posters just two days ago. By noon, we had thirty-five more posters, and a new article had been emailed to several local papers. I carried a box full of posters home, gulped some lunch, said goodbye to Solow and drove over the mountain to Gilroy.

As I tried to cover all the shopping areas and neighborhoods with posters, I ran into several hostile shop owners who said they didn't want paper and rubbish attached to their buildings. Some didn't want tape, some didn't want tack holes and some had vagrants lounging on their sidewalks and wanted nothing to do with our program. But most shop owners were thrilled that something was being done, and they were hoping the race would help the homeless to get on their feet and off the sidewalks.

With just five more posters left in the box, my phone rang.

"Oh, hi, David."

"Where are you, Josephine?"

"Gilroy...."

"I have a list of things I need for tomorrow."

"Okay, fire away," I said, digging in my purse for a pen and something to write on. He rattled off eight different things including a couple of spices I had never heard of. I told him not to worry. I would find everything.

Nob Hill Market had everything, plus my own personal shopper to find it all. The nice checker left his ten-items-or-less station and found one item after another for me. Everything except the butter and sour cream, because I knew where to find them.

On my way home, I stopped at the nursery and taped up my last poster on a wall inside the gift shop.

"Caitlin, where are Bea and Jason?"

"Jason will be back from a delivery soon, but Bea hasn't been in today."

"Did you check the tool shed?"

"Huh?"

"Never mind. Caitlin, would you and Lito like to come to turkey dinner tomorrow at my fiancé's house?"

She glanced at the floor and smiled. "Actually, I'm going to have Thanksgiving with my family—Chico and Lito. We're going to give it a try."

"That's wonderful, I hope it works out for you."

"Thank you, Josephine." Big girl-hug.

Remembering that I needed to get the cold foods over to David's fridge before they warmed up, I left the nursery and began my drive back to Aromas. As my sweet little truck chugged up the mountain, my eyes wandered to the left side of the road where a tiny seasonal river tumbled downhill between high riverbanks. Hecker Pass Road mimicked the sharp turns of the narrow gorge, staying close to its leafy, mulchy banks.

A few more fall leaves fluttered downward, helpless against the will of the wind. Tiny specks of sky peeked through a heavy canopy of evergreen trees, namely redwoods, and splotches of bright green moss clung to tree trunks and rotting logs. It was all so mysteriously beautiful that I almost didn't see a familiar-looking car parked on the right side of the road, the side with no pullover room.

I tugged the wheel and hit the brake, but still managed to wing the little hatchback. I pulled to a stop against the embankment a few feet in front of the car and jumped out to see if anyone was around. There was Bea, sitting behind the wheel taking a nap.

"Wait a minute," I said to myself, "nobody takes a nap sticking out in the road...."

A car whooshed around the turn and sped up the grade.

Bea's head lolled against the headrest, mouth open, eyes shut.

"Bea, wake up...wake up!" I pushed on her shoulder. She didn't move. I felt the pulses in her neck and wrist. They were barely there. Quickly, heart racing, I dashed up to my truck, grabbed my phone and called 911.

A blue delivery truck slowed on its downhill journey but kept going.

Too panicked to notice who stopped to help and who didn't, all I knew was that Bea looked pale and her breathing was shallow. In no time, three cars were parked along the other side of the road. One concerned citizen crossed the two-lane highway and asked if I needed help, just seconds before we heard sirens.

Bea was put on a gurney and shipped off to Gilroy, that being the closest town for medical help. I fired up my truck, made a u-turn and followed the ambulance as far as the nursery where I notified Caitlin and asked her to pass the Bea news on to Jason.

By the time I got to the hospital, worked my way through the emergency room medical maze and found Bea's room, she was already hooked up to fluids and oxygen. Nurses bustled in, out and around. One of them pointed to the hall.

Taking the nurse's suggestion, I found a waiting room with a vending machine. Once I was settled in with a cup of hot coffee and a Snickers bar, I called David.

He said he planned to make the turkey dressing ahead and bake pumpkin pies and an apricot pie when the spices and other ingredients arrived.

"Looks like I won't be home for a while...." I said.

"Don't worry, Josie, I'll make the pies tomorrow morning. I have to get up early anyway to roast the turkey. Just let me know how your friend is getting along."

"I'll call you when I know more about it. Love you."

We hung up and I called Sugarbell.

"Hello, sorry, Josephine, I can't...."

"Sugarbell, don't hang up. It's about your mother."

"I'm working, but what about Mom?"

"She's in the hospital in Gilroy. I found her asleep in her car...."

"Oh God, I think she took her medicine."

"I thought you wanted her to take it...."

"Sometimes she forgets she took it and takes it again. Tell the doctor it's probably an antidepressant overdose. I'll be right down there—thank you, Josephine."

Back in Bea's room, I walked up to a man wearing a stethoscope around his scrawny neck. His eyes were focused on a monitor on the wall behind Bea's bed. Breaking into the doctor's concentration was awkward, but he finally listened to me. He gave me a nod of his head, letting me know that the imparted information might be helpful.

Ten minutes later I sat with Sugarbell in the waiting room, filling her in on what happened. The scrawny-neck doctor entered the room and took Sugarbell aside.

I wasn't sure who had the most to say, but she walked with him down the hall to her mother's room. Alone with my warm coffee, I asked God to forgive my former bad thoughts toward Bea and to please wake her up.

A tall woman wearing an ankle-length black wool coat walked into the little waiting room and stood in front of the TV.

"Oh, it's you, Fern. I thought you were in jail."

"You wish. If it's any of your business, I have a court date. My word against yours," she grinned. "How's my stupid sister doing?"

"I don't know...." I said.

"Now that I found you, Josephine, I want my hat and scarf."

"You're right, they'd look nice with your coat." I laughed at the nasty woman. "But they would clash with your orange overalls in jail."

"If I don't get them, something bad is going to happen," she sneered.

"I can't help you because I don't have them...."

"If you love that stupid dog of yours, you'll get me the hat and scarf." Fern stood up and stormed out of the building without even checking on Bea.

A chill ran through my body. Could she actually hurt my sweet Solow? Maybe I should give her what she wanted but secretly arrange to have the police on hand to arrest her.

Sugarbell came back and sat with me. She had peeked in at her mom, but the doctor told her he would notify her as soon as Bea was awake.

"Are you okay, Josephine? You look so sad. Mom's going to be all right according to the doctor."

"Actually I was thinking about your Aunt Fern. She was just here."

"And she didn't even go see my mom—just like her! I don't know why I bothered to call her," Sugarbell lamented.

We fell into a conversation about the upcoming race and all the other events that had sprung up around it. Only three days left to train. Maybe another hike up to Molly's would help me get into shape. Sugarbell was in great shape, but she wouldn't run because she would be busy at the finish line handing out t-shirts to the first three finishers, first place, oldest finisher and the youngest.

An hour later, the doctor walked up to Sugarbell and told her that her mother was stable.

I said goodbye to Sugarbell and headed out to the hospital parking lot.

A tall, dark man climbed out of an Uber car and handed the driver some money. He walked over to the sidewalk where I stood, waiting for traffic to let me cross the parking lot.

"Hey, Josephine, leaving already?"

"Hi, Rico, Bea is okay. I have to run some cold groceries home before they spoil. See ya."

"Yeah, later." He headed into the building, and I fast-walked to my truck.

All the way home, I thought about Fern threatening to hurt Solow. Could she do such a thing? I knew that she knew where I lived. My mind bounced from one terrible scenario to another. In the end, I decided I would arrange a meeting with Fern, give her the hat and scarf and have the police waiting to grab her as she left with the goods. But first, I would check out the knitted items to see where the stolen chip was hidden.

It was already dark when I drove through Aromas, and my stomach growled that it was hungry. I thought about David waiting for me to come home, lighting a fire in the wood stove and turning on the porch light. A block from home I already smelled wood smoke from the chimney. I smiled at the thought of an evening with David, popcorn and a movie.

The wood smell became stronger as I turned up my driveway and braked behind a fire engine. White smoke poured from the kitchen window.

Chapter 24

I opened my eyes and realized that the nightmare was real. I had all but ruined Thanksgiving Day for David, his family and mine. He didn't blame me, but he didn't understand either. David didn't understand why my oven was full of newspaper and such. He barely understood why I was so late with the groceries and he didn't like my plan to pretend to give Fern the hat and scarf. However, he did like one aspect of the plan...the police standing by.

An acrid odor wafted into my bedroom, reminding me again of the mess in the kitchen. David had explained that he had two large pans of turkey dressing baking in his oven and he was preheating my oven for an apricot pie. He opened the oven door to insert the pie, but the inside of the oven suddenly caught fire. The pie and some flaming debris landed on the floor. David slammed the oven door shut. Unfortunately, hot pieces of burning material had already licked at my cupboards and then up the wall.

David said that a fire engine had arrived quickly, but not before the oven was ruined, the wall blackened and the linoleum pockmarked with holes burned into it from falling debris. Not to mention David's singed eyebrows.

Trying hard to forget the whole episode, I took a warm shower and drank a mug of coffee. Eventually my mood improved a bit. Solow stayed with me, sensing my misery and reminding me that I needed to talk to Fern before she did something horrible to my dog. I dialed her number.

"Josephine, have you come to your senses?" Fern asked.

"I've decided to make a deal...."

"No deal. Just get those things to me," she snapped.

"Okay, but I can't get them to you until Friday. Meet me at six o'clock at the Aromas Grange...."

"Why there?" Fern demanded.

"Because it's a public place, and I don't want any funny business."

"All right, Josephine, but I warn you. Come alone. And I don't want to see that stupid dog of yours."

She hung up.

I told Solow not to worry. It would be dark by six o'clock, and the cops would be a block away and out of sight. I shared my bacon and eggs with him, and we both felt better.

Mom called to ask if she could use my oven. Her green bean casserole would need to be reheated. Their plan was to come to my house around eleven and we would all go over to David's at two. The turkey was scheduled to be done by three.

"Actually, my oven is out of order right now," I explained.

"What does that mean? Do you want Bob to work on it?"

"No, Mom, you'll see what I mean when you get here. Better yet, why don't you go straight to David's at one o'clock and I'll meet you there?"

"But, dear, I think Myrtle was looking forward to seeing your place. She hasn't been there in years," Mom said.

"Well, things around here are a little run-down. She might be disappointed. I'll see you at David's at one. Love you, bye." I hung up, held my breath, but Mom didn't call back.

The day was grey and cool. I opened the windows anyway. Fresh air poured in until my goose bumps and I couldn't take it any more. I set up a six-foot ladder and began scrubbing the kitchen ceiling with soapy water. When the ceiling was finished, I changed the water and scrubbed the cabinets. By ten o'clock, I had finished cleaning the floor, pockmarks and all. It was obvious that the room needed a major makeover.

I used the tension in my shoulders plus tight calf muscles as my excuse for a walk up the road with Solow. Without thinking, we ended up at Molly's. She answered her door wearing a purple bathrobe and fuzzy matching slippers.

"Josephine, what a surprise—and dear Solow." Molly bent down to rub his ears. "What's going on?"

"I was wondering what you do around here before the Thanksgiving dinner...."

"Watch the parade on TV, of course." She motioned for us to come inside. "Would you like a piece of spice cake? I made it from scratch," she smiled.

"Molly, why don't you bring the cake down to David's house for Thanksgiving dinner? I think we're going to need an extra dessert."

Molly seemed happy to be able to contribute to the meal.

"What time should I be there?"

"Why don't you come over around two, that way you can finish watching the parade and take your time getting ready—but it will be casual."

Would she wear sweats? It didn't matter. The main thing was to have her meet the families and enjoy the food. Besides, the spice cake sounded good.

Leaving Molly's, I glanced over at Jason's house. I didn't see one car or truck on the property, not even Caitlin's truck. I knew they weren't working at the nursery because it was closed for the holiday. As I watched, Jason's little white dog limped around the corner of the house.

Solow pulled on his leash in the direction of the little dog across the street. I followed him up the driveway, but the little dog had already disappeared. We strolled along a concrete path leading to the backyard, Solow sniffing the sidewalk like an anteater with a cold. As we turned left and cornered the back of the house, I craned my neck and looked up to the second story where an ornate Spanish-style railing ringed a small balcony jutting out from a wall of sliding glass doors. The sight made me shutter. I looked down at my feet, which were partially covering a dark stain on the concrete, and jumped back a couple of feet.

The least the family could do would be to remove the stain left by their dying mother's blood.

The little white dog doubled back and peeked around the corner, testing to see if Solow was friend or foe. Minutes later, they had sniffed each other from north to south and back again—just a couple of friends getting together.

After a few attempts at petting the little thing, he finally let me pat him on his head. The gimpy leg had a strange angle to it. No wonder it didn't work. It looked like it had been broken, and then healed that way. Vaguely, I remembered Jason saying that his mother had kicked the dog. Except for a gimpy leg, the dog seemed to be more normal than anyone else in the Oeblick family.

Solow and I walked to the opposite back corner of the house and turned left. Twenty yards away stood the cottage where Caitlin and Lito lived. We walked along a garden path, crossed an empty two-vehicle parking area and peeked in the cottage's front room window. The place was one hundred percent empty.

I smiled and said to Solow, "Looks like Caitlin and Lito have gone home to their Papa. We need to go home and get ready for the big dinner at David's."

Entering my house, the sour smoky air smell could not be ignored. After opening windows and doors and setting the bathroom and stove fans in motion, I squirted Windex on every surface and wiped until my arm ached. By noon, the place smelled like a hospital, cold and sanitary.

Ignoring my instructions, Mom, Dad and Myrtle showed up on my front porch at twelve o'clock. I was still wearing my grubby sweats and tennis shoes. I opened the door and took Myrtle's casserole from her shaky hands. Mom and Dad each carried a covered side dish through the house to the kitchen.

"Don't worry, dear, we just need to warm these before the meal," Mom said.

"Like I said over the phone, the oven is out of order."

"Your father is very good at fixing things...."

"I'm telling you it won't work." I turned away and rolled my eyes up to a few persistent grey smudges on the ceiling.

Mom set her dish on the counter and opened the oven door as if she could diagnose what the problem was. She sniffed the air and commented that the interior of the oven was as black as a coal mine and smelled sour. She suggested it might just need a good cleaning. Her eyes latched onto a portion of cupboard door above the oven that was deeply singed. Her mouth dropped open. She was starting to get the picture.

"Mom, I didn't tell you about the fire because I didn't want to worry you...."

Suddenly looking pale, she said, "Honey, you can always tell me these things." Her voice faded into a whisper.

"It was just one of those things. I was hiding something wrapped in newspaper...."

"In the oven?" Dad blurted.

"Yeah, temporarily, but David didn't know it was in there," I explained, suddenly feeling hot enough to jump into an arctic snowdrift.

All three of them looked at me like I must have been an alien baby that rode a meteor down to their front porch fifty years ago.

"David's oven had two big pans of dressing in it, so he came over here to bake his apricot pie."

Everyone seemed to be horrified over the fact that my oven didn't work. I looked at it like a vacation from baking, cheerful person that I am. I poured cups of coffee for everyone and then excused myself from the roomful of quizzical looks and comments. Once I was in my bedroom, I took my time shedding my jeans and t-shirt, and changing into a nice sweater and slacks outfit. By the time I joined my folks and Myrtle, I had an idea.

"Don't you look lovely, dear," Myrtle cooed.

"It's about time," Mom said, as Dad elbowed her.

"How would you guys like to meet the people in charge of Saturday's race?" I said.

They didn't exactly beat a path to the door, but they all looked interested. A few minutes later, we were in Mom's Subaru heading east on Hecker Pass Road.

Going up they marveled at the panoramic views, and going down they loved the beautiful forest along the eastern face of the mountain. Myrtle said she hadn't traveled through the forest since she was a young woman. I wondered if she had traveled by car or horse and buggy.

I had called Sugarbell before we left Aromas. She gave me directions to St. Joseph's Family Center in Gilroy where she would be with her friends. We arrived at the corner of First and Church streets and parked in the back. We followed the smell of turkey and pie into a large back room. At least fifty people were lined up to receive a plate of food. Myrtle positioned herself behind a mom and her two little kids, making her last in line.

Mom and Dad had other ideas. When I introduced them to Sugarbell, they asked her how they could be of help. She pointed to mashed potatoes for Mom and carving turkeys for Dad. I filled the salad slot, a scoop of greens on each plate.

"No thank ya, ma'am," an old gentleman said, as his plate passed from the gravy station to my station. He wore everything he owned, layered until he looked twice his real size.

"Salads are good for you…." I said, raising a spoonful to his plate.

"Girl food. Git it off my plate."

"All right already. Have a nice day." I handed him his plate. The next person in line was a woman somewhere between thirty and sixty. She obviously had been in the sun quite a bit since her skin had big wrinkles and folds in it. Like the gentleman, she also wore layers of clothing, topped off with an off-white knitted cap and a long matching scarf wrapped around her neck.

"I like salad," she smiled. "I'll take another scoop please."

"Well, okay…what would you take for that hat and scarf?"

"What?"

"The hat and scarf. I want to buy them from you," I said, as the gal behind her checked her wardrobe to see if she too could sell something.

"Ha, ha, I'd have to charge you twenty bucks…."

"Okay, it's a deal," I said.

She looked at me with wide eyes. "And five dollars more because my sons coming to town and I want to give him a bottle, I mean a good time."

"Maybe he'd like to go to a movie," I suggested to the lady with dollar signs in her eyes.

She smiled at me like a river rat smiles at a cockroach.

"I'll find your table in ten minutes."

She nodded and moved down the line.

I slopped salad on plates for another ten minutes.

Mom took over my spot plus working the mashed potatoes and gravy station, while I grabbed my purse and found the hat and scarf lady. She looked up from her meal.

"Will you take a check?" I asked.

"And what would I do with that?"

"Oh, sorry." I handed her twenty-five dollars in cash. "The hat...."

"Oh yeah, here ya go," she said, as she pulled the cap off her head and unwound the scarf. She handed the items to me. I thanked her and went back to the kitchen. Pungent turkey and pie smells filled the air, but my new garments smelled strongly of wood smoke and something sour. Before I handed them over to Fern, I would have to wash them and dye them turquoise.

And then I remembered that we had left Solow home alone.

Chapter 25

It was a miracle that my folks, Myrtle and I made it back to Aromas by two-thirty. Sugarbell had wanted us to stay at St. Joseph's longer, and Mom and Dad were really enthusiastic about their work. Myrtle became involved in a discussion with three homeless women who said they had lived that way for over five years. I reminded them that dinner would soon be served at David's house.

The second miracle was finding a hat and scarf to give to Fern. All I had to do was launder and dye them. If Ted showed up with Fern, all bets where off. The thought of him made my knees go weak. But that worry was for tomorrow.

I hadn't planned to help David prepare the Thanksgiving dinner because he could cook circles around me. I figured I would just be in the way. But Mom jumped right in and began setting the table for eight, and Dad began mashing the boiled potatoes energetically. Harley worked in the backyard barbecuing sausages while Molly arranged the various salads and hot dishes on the island counter. Myrtle and I stood ready to handle odd jobs like helping Monica find Mr. Bunny, and opening the occasional pickle jar.

David announced that everything was ready and to please fill our plates at the island counter. I picked up a plate, but couldn't fill it. Something was missing. I let everyone go ahead of me. I looked around at the table and realized that Solow was home alone. It was traditional for him to be under the table in case a piece of food fell to the floor.

I told David I would be right back and slipped out the back door.

Cutting through the acres of grass separating our two houses, I pictured Solow romping after Fluffy. Under November's dry spent grass, two-inch sprouts of green grass pressed upward. By December, everything would be green. Unfortunately, the old grass was loaded with stickers, and they loved to work their way into my socks and pant legs.

As I walked across my patio and approached the back door, all was quiet. Solow must be asleep, I thought. I turned the knob and entered my well-scrubbed kitchen.

"Solow, come."

I walked through the house calling him but to no avail. Had I left him outside? I stepped out the front door and called again and again. An ugly idea occurred to me. Maybe Fern dognapped Solow to make sure she got her knits. My head felt dizzy and my heart raced. Tears streamed down my cheeks as I headed back to David's house.

Entering the dining room, I noticed that everyone was holding hands, waiting for me to sit down before saying a short prayer. I quickly slid into my chair, and when grace was done, I took my plate to the island buffet and filled it. The last thing I wanted to do was eat, but I pushed my food around and made a good show of complimenting the cooks.

David sat at the head of the table, and I sat opposite him. He gave me strange looks as I tried to look normal.

"So, you didn't want to disturb Solow?" David said, his eyes drilling into me. I knew that he knew that something was wrong. But if I talked about it, I would lose control for sure.

"Something like that." A lump had formed in my throat.

Mom sat at my right elbow. "Aren't you hungry, dear?" she whispered.

"I'm saving myself for David's apricot pie and Molly's spice cake."

Perky little Monica sat at my left elbow. "I ate all my food so I can have pie. If you don't eat everything, Grandpa says you can't have pie."

She was the cutest little redhead, but something in me wanted to roll up a newspaper and smack her with it. Instead, I leaned closer and kissed her forehead.

"Your face is wet," Monica said.

I quickly dried the tears with my napkin, and stuffed a chunk of sweet potato into my mouth. Trying hard not to ruin Thanksgiving, I was ruining it. Everyone at the table gave me curious glances, making it harder and harder to hold my emotions steady. I heard a familiar tune coming from my purse in the other room. I ignored it. The phone quit for a few minutes, then started up again. I excused myself and went to take care of it.

Snatching up the phone, I carried it outside.

"Not answering your phone won't help you to get your dog back," Fern said.

"You hurt my dog and you'll be in bad shape when I get done with you."

"What are you going to do to me?" she laughed. "You'll get your old mutt back when I see you tomorrow—if I get what I want."

"You will," I growled. I walked into the dining room, and everyone stopped chewing and looked up. "I need to go check on Solow. He's not feeling well." I turned and hurried through the house and out the front door. The cold outside air sharpened my thoughts. I knew what I had to do.

It was almost five and almost dark as I worked my way across the field to my house. Collecting up a jacket, flashlight and a bottle of water, I was ready to leave Thanksgiving behind. My first stop would be St. Joseph's. I had plenty of time to think, as I drove over the mountain to Gilroy, but I didn't change my mind. I was dead set on getting my dog back and hoped that Sugarbell would help me.

I parked my truck behind the church and fast-walked to the back door of the old Spanish-style building where half a dozen grocery carts piled high with people's belongings were parked.

Out of the corner of my eye, something moved.

"Can I help you?" a man asked, dressed in layers of hoodies and dark clothing, sitting in a folding chair next to the carts.

"I'm looking for Sugarbell...."

"Oh, she took a break, but she be back in a few minutes. She gonna check on her Mama."

"Is Bea still in the hospital?"

He shrugged. "I dunno."

"Thanks," I said and ran back to my truck.

My phone rang.

I ignored it. Number one, it was illegal to hold a cell phone while driving and number two, I was in no mood to chitchat with anyone. From the church, I headed west a mile or so to Tiller Road and Holiday Park. As soon as I climbed out of my seat, I smelled wood smoke and heard muffled voices from the homeless camp. Trudging across the meadow in the dark, I headed west toward the river and the faint light from a bonfire. Eventually I came close enough to make out silhouettes of people standing around, trying to keep warm. Sugarbell was one of them.

"Josephine, welcome to our fire...."

"Hi, Sugarbell, can I talk to you alone?"

"Yeah, I guess so." She moved away from the fire and whispered, "What's the problem?"

"Your Aunt Fern has dognapped Solow...." I felt my lips quiver.

"That's terrible. How can I help?" she asked, even though she was probably exhausted from a full day's work serving the homeless at the church.

"I need a distraction...I'll explain on the way to Morgan Hill."

"Where in Morgan Hill?'"

"Your aunt's house on Hill Street. Do you still want to help?"

"More than ever," she said, as she turned and said goodbye to her friends.

On the way to Morgan Hill, Sugarbell answered my questions about Bea, telling me how her mother was resting in her tent and glad to be alive. She said that Bea had promised to take her medicine responsibly, and she would let Sugarbell manage her recovery for a while.

I filled Sugarbell in on my plan to get Solow back. It was a partial plan. I hoped the rest of it would be clear in my mind by the time we arrived at Fern's door.

I curbed the truck half a block downhill from Fern's house because my downhill running was better than my uphill speed if we had to race back to the truck for any reason.

We sat staring at the neighborhood. Not a soul around. I dialed 911.

"911, what's your emergency?"

"My friend and I are at 4000 Hill Street in Morgan Hill, and two people are painting the outside of the house."

"At night?" she asked.

"Yeah, you know, graffiti," I said.

"Do you feel safe where you are?"

"Um, not really," I lied.

"I'll see if we can send a car out—hold on." A minute went by. "Ma'am, a sheriff will be out there in twenty to thirty minutes."

"Okay, but no siren."

"Right," she said. "Stay on the phone until the car arrives."

I promised I would and stuck the phone in my pants pocket.

"Why didn't you just say that someone stole your dog?"

"The last time someone stole my dog I didn't get any help, so I thought we could commit a crime the police would pay attention to."

Sugarbell didn't look convinced, but she was being a good sport. We talked about the race coming up in two days. She said she had been asking around for a starting pistol but hadn't found one yet. I told her I would try to locate one for her.

The minutes passed slowly. After ten minutes of sitting around, we climbed out of the truck, and I popped open the bed top. We pulled out my paint box and a couple of brushes and hiked up the sidewalk. Hill Street had streetlights, so we had no trouble seeing our way along the sidewalk, but people could see us if they happened to look out a window. But Fern's shades were down, and my adrenaline was pumping. We carried the paint to Fern's sidewall facing the street and set up shop. I used black paint and Sugarbell used red.

I wrote, "Fern has my dog" in large letters across the light beige stucco.

Sugarbell wrote, "Please help Solow."

And then I wrote, "Ted tried to kill me."

Hill Street was dead quiet.

Headlights came up the hill behind us. We ducked behind a large bush. A black and white cruiser overshot the house, turned around and parked across the street. Two people in the car watched the house for five long minutes while the bush tickled and poked us.

Two city policemen climbed out of their vehicle and sauntered over to our graffiti.

"Dumb son of a gun can't spell. What's a Solow? A planet?"

"It's the dog's name. This paint is still wet!"

Did you hear something?" one of them asked.

"Excuse me," I said as nicely as I could.

"Who's there?" the tall first cop demanded, as he drew his gun.

Sugarbell and I stepped out from behind the bush with our hands in the air.

"Don't tell me you ladies did this!" the short second cop said, sounding like a disappointed parent.

"We needed to get you up here—it was the only way. My dog is inside this house, and Sugarbell's aunt is the one who stole him. She went right in my house and took him. Too bad he didn't bite her...."

"Ma'am, what proof do you have?" Slim asked.

Shorty stepped closer. "Why would she take your dog?"

I started to tell them the story, but they insisted we go sit in the back seat of the cruiser.

We went willingly.

They climbed in the front, and we all had a lengthy chat. When they were about seventy percent convinced, I threw in the fact that Fern was under investigation for stealing chips from the company she worked for. They looked at each other and decided to check it out.

We were locked in the back seat. No amount of protesting worked to get us out. We watched the two policemen cross Hill Street and ring Fern's doorbell. We couldn't even open a window, but I thought I heard the faint bark of a dog.

Chapter 26

Friday Morning I awoke to Solow's melodic snoring. Having him back was worth all the explaining and apologizing I had had to do to my family and friends. I had missed the best parts of Thanksgiving—especially pie—but knowing that Fern and Ted were behind bars had a soothing effect on my nerves.

Even after yesterday's good outcome, something nagged at me. It was like leaving for a trip out-of-town knowing that you forgot something, but you can't think what it is no matter how hard you try. But you have a feeling it's something important. In the middle of breakfast, I remembered what I had forgotten. I had been so busy dealing with the homeless, knits, Solow and Fern that I forgot to follow my instincts concerning Mrs. Oeblick's murder. Ever since I saw her blood stain below the balcony, I knew I had to keep looking for the person who killed her.

When Sugarbell and I were released from the back of the squad car so that Ted and Fern could take our places, Fern cussed and screamed at us. Her last words were, "You're always mess'n with my family, and you still don't know who did it," she cackled.

I knew Fern was talking about her mother's murder. It sounded like the murder could have been committed by one of her family members…but which one? If it was Bea, Fern would have happily turned her into the police long ago. But she seemed to get along pretty well with her brothers. Was it one of them?

My goal for the day was to finish painting the bucking horse and check some records at the nursery. Solow came to work with me. He needed to be close, and I needed to know that he was safe at all times of the day. I painted the nursery wall just a couple of feet from where he lay on the pavement under a weak winter sun. Caitlin puttered around the nursery wearing a smile, while Jason loaded the delivery truck with several out-of-town orders.

The instant Jason's truck roared onto Hecker Pass Road, I dropped my brush in the water bucket and headed over to the gift shop with Solow at my heels. I told Caitlin I would take over so she could have a break. She happily walked out to her truck, cell phone in hand and husband on the line.

Alone in the shop, I opened a drawer under the register and thumbed through receipts going back to July. Mrs. Oeblick had been murdered on October 31, Halloween, an easy date to remember. I finally found receipts from October, and then one from October 31. Jason had signed it. A nursery in Aptos had ordered six miniature palm trees and two rose bushes. I double-checked the pile for October, but that was the only delivery for October 31.

I slipped the receipt into my pocket and looked up. There stood an older gentleman holding a deep-red potted chrysanthemum against his buttoned, plaid flanneled chest. His eyes squinted as if to say, "Does your boss know you took that receipt?"

"Hello, can I help you?" I said with all the charm I could muster on quick notice.

He placed the chrysanthemum on the counter.

"I'll ring it up, Josephine," Caitlin said, as she walked to the register. Her phone call must have been a good one because her face was glowing.

"Thanks, I'll be outside painting if you need me."

Caitlin didn't need me. She buzzed around the property watering plants, putting away tools and ringing up customers while I painted. Three hours later, the horse had dimension, muscles and a shiny coat. I really liked the way the horse turned out, but dreaded painting the rider. What if the rider turned out to be the murderer? That's when I decided to put it off till another day.

As I packed up my paint gear, Jason's truck pulled into the parking lot. He cut the engine and hopped down from his seat.

"Josephine, you're going home?"

"Yeah, I'll paint your image on the horse tomorrow morning when I'm fresh."

"Chester looks great. I miss that old horse," he said.

"By the way, Jason, any chance you can pay me for my time up to now?"

"No problem. Give me a minute to write a check."

I followed Jason to the gift shop. He wrote the check and handed it to me. I thanked him and went back to my truck where Solow waited in the passenger seat. We headed into Gilroy looking for a quick lunch. Without even thinking, we ended up at the hot dog place where Sugarbell worked. From the take-out window, she told me she was due for a break in ten minutes and would join us in the parking lot.

Ten minutes later, Sugarbell opened the passenger door and climbed in.

"You have mustard on your jacket, Josephine."

"Thanks." I dipped a napkin into my coke and smeared the mustard around until it was almost gone.

"I've been wanting to talk to you, but usually there are people around. I know that you're actively looking for my grandmother's killer."

"Do you think it was someone you know?" I asked.

"Might be...."

"Someone in your family?"

"Probably," she muttered, looking down at her folded hands.

Solow had curled his body around Sugarbell's feet. He stared up at her from his tight space under the dash.

"My Uncle Jason is a good guy, but he told the sheriff he wasn't home that night."

"Anyone else in the family you suspect?"

"Fern was there, but she was my grandma's favorite," Sugarbell said.

"Anyone else?" I asked.

"I don't know what to think. I like my uncles, but Rico hasn't exactly been truthful. I was at my grandmother's house a week after Halloween when he was being questioned by two officers. He told them he hadn't been to Aromas until that day. Josephine, I was at the house Halloween night. He was there—dressed as a pirate. Actually most of the guests were pirates."

She dropped her chin for a moment, then took a deep breath.

"That does sound suspicious. So the family was there for a costume party?"

"Yes, but not everyone wore a costume. Mom and I opted out."

"Did the murder happen while you were there?"

"Oh no, Mom and I left around eight o'clock. Fern said she and Ted didn't leave until midnight, and Molly and Fred were there all that time along with Caitlin and Lito plus some of Jason's friends from Fresno who were staying the night. I'd say there were at least twenty people all together."

"The Molly you're talking about, would that be Jason's neighbor across the street?" I felt my blood turn cold.

"Yep—sorry, Josephine, I gotta run." Sugarbell leaped out of her seat and slammed the door. Two minutes later, her pretty face looked out from the drive-up window. She waved to us.

I couldn't finish eating my last hot dog so I gave it to Solow. He sat on the seat looking out the window as I drove to Aromas. We rolled through town and turned onto Otis. Solow howled when we drove right past my house plus twelve mailboxes, eventually pulling into Molly's driveway.

I rang the bell and Molly answered the door.

"Hi, Molly, can I come in?"

"Of course. And Solow's here," she grinned.

We sat down on the well-pillowed sofa. "Molly, do you know someone named Fred?"

"My brother's name is Fred...I think he's the only Fred I know."

"Did you go to Jason's Halloween party with Fred?"

"How did you...ah, yeah, we were wearing really cool pirate costumes that my brother rented."

"Pirates?"

"Yeah, it was a Pirates of the Caribbean theme." Her brow wrinkled.

"So where was Mrs. Oeblick all this time?" I asked.

"She stayed in her room, knitting. She was in the last stages of cancer—at least that's what Jason told me. Even without cancer, she would never join a party." Molly examined her thumbnail.

"How do you know she was knitting?"

Molly looked at me, blinking her eyes. The eyes became wet as her face caved and her tight lips twisted. I knew we were on the brink of a confession. Molly looked relieved as she spilled out all her Halloween night secrets. She had left her brother downstairs playing darts with Jason, Rico and a couple other guys. The downstair's restroom was being used so she headed upstairs to a bathroom adjoining Mrs. Oeblick's bedroom.

As Molly went about her business, she heard a dog crying. She opened the door into the old lady's room and saw the woman throw a little white dog off her bed.

The dog yipped, shook itself and stood up on three legs.

The old woman screamed at it in another language.

Without thinking, Molly rushed through the bedroom and out onto the small balcony where the dog shivered in fear.

Mrs. Oeblick put her knitting aside, except for one needle, and climbed out of her bed. Molly watched her stumble onto the balcony brandishing one long knitting needle. The old woman tried to pull the dog from Molly's arms but Molly held tight. Finally Molly set the dog down, but it instantly fell over on its side when the old lady kicked it with her bare foot.

Mrs. Oeblick gave Molly a tongue lashing. When she was finished, she spit on her nosey neighbor. Molly automatically slapped the old woman in the face, just before the knitting needle found its mark, and the struggle began. One woman hit the pavement and one walked away, blood dripping from her shoulder, hardly able to comprehend what had just happened. But from the sound of Mrs. Oeblick's head hitting the concrete sidewalk, Molly knew the woman was already heading into another dimension.

By the end of Molly's confession, she was bawling her eyes out.

"It's okay, Molly, get it all out of your system."

"I'm a murderer..." she blubbered.

"No, you're not. Yes, you should have walked away, but in the end you were just trying to protect a helpless little dog and yourself." I silently wondered if her case would come to trial. If it did, would the jury take pity on her?

"Shall I call, or do you want to?" I said.

"I'll do it. I've dreaded this moment for weeks, but now I actually feel like a huge weight has been lifted from my shoulders. No more lies and no more nightmares."

Molly reached for the phone and dialed 911.

Epilogue

The Oeblick family had its problems, but some things were improving like Bea's personality when she took her medicine. Jason gave her a raise and she moved into an apartment with Sugarbell.

Jason moved into his former home in Gilroy, and his dad settled into the homestead at the end of Otis Road with his lovely nurse. Daphne ran off to Mexico with Ted, Rico moved back to Brazil and Fern waited for her trial.

Molly waited for her trial date, but her lawyer-brother, Fred, told her not to worry. It looked like a case of self-defense since Mrs. Oeblick had attacked her with a sharp knitting needle. Molly still had a scar from the puncture wound to prove it.

The town of Gilroy and its homeless population benefited greatly from the funds raised by the race/walkathon and all the events surrounding it. Mr. Eze from Kenya was first across the finish line. Leola finished four-hundred and fiftieth, but first in the over-seventy class.

When Josephine knew for sure that Jason was not the murderer, she was finally able to paint a handsome cowboy riding the bucking horse she had already painted on the nursery warehouse wall.

Josephine finished her work at the nursery and had seven more days until she and Alicia were scheduled to paint murals at the Gilroy Library. David thought it would be nice to take his sweetheart north to the wine

country for a few days. Josephine knew that was exactly what she need.

THE END

ABOUT THE AUTHOR

 Author Joyce Oroz keeps a busy schedule, balancing her writing projects with family and social engagements plus therapeutic time working in her garden. Oroz recently decided to write a true story about a Farm School created in the sixties to help children with mental and physical disabilities learn practical life skills. The story involves one child's tragedy, progress and eventual joy, as told through her teachers, Loreen and Sena.

The author's newest book is an illustrated children's story dealing with separation anxiety as demonstrated through a young dog left alone each weekday as her family goes off to work and school. The name of the book is, *"Annie Gets Her Bounce."* It is available on Amazon.

Coming soon will be Oroz's non-fiction, how-to book, *"Muraling for Fun and Profit."* This book is 20% about painting and 80% about turning the love of painting into a well-paid mural business. Before she wrote her first book, Joyce Oroz had a life-long love of painting, which she turned into a lucrative business. These days she finds it easier to write about painting in her mystery books, letting Josephine do all the work.